Crystal Saga Series 4

3 — The New Order
4 — Adapting to Change

D. E. Weingand

Crystal Saga Series 4

3 – The New Order
4 – Adapting to Change
A Crystal Saga Series

ISBN: 979-8-218-47756-1

Published by D. E. Weingand, Florence, Oregon 97439.

Printed in the United States of America.

Front cover photo by D. E. Weingand. Design by Luanna K. Leisure.

Luanna K. Leisure, Little White Feather Graphic Designer, and Independent Publisher. Campbell, California.

To order additional books go to: **http://www.LuLu.com, Amazon.com or Barnesandnoble.com**
Email: weingand@me.com

The New Order
Crystal Saga Series 4
Book 3

Table of Contents

Book 3

Table of Contents Continued

Adapting to Change
Crystal Saga Series 4
Book 4

Table of Contents

AKURA

LIGHT SIDE

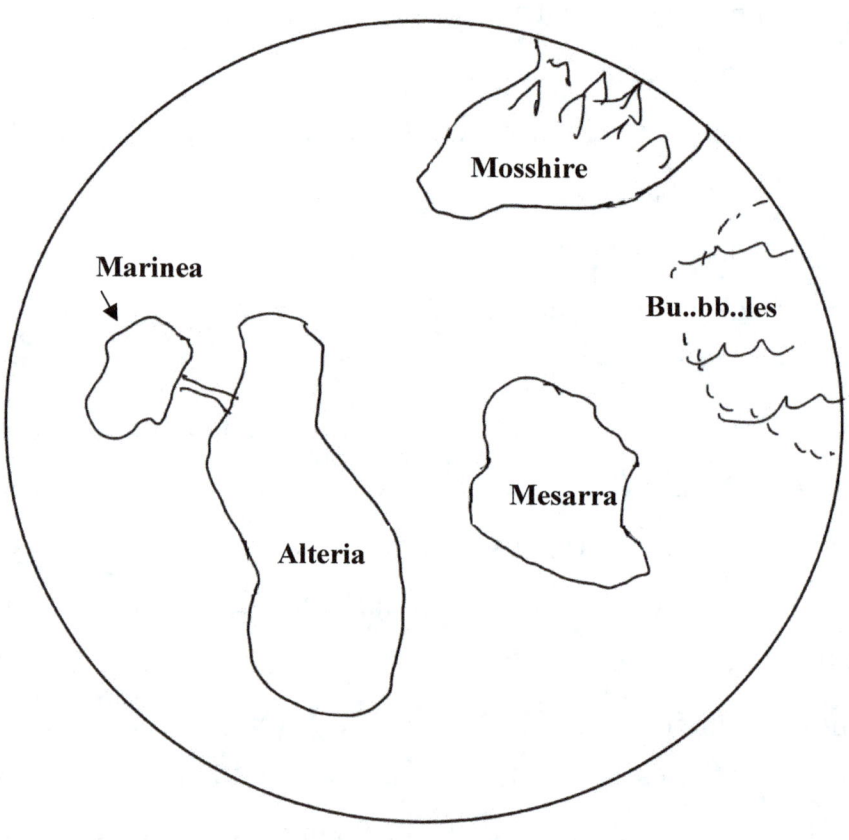

AKURA
DARK SIDE

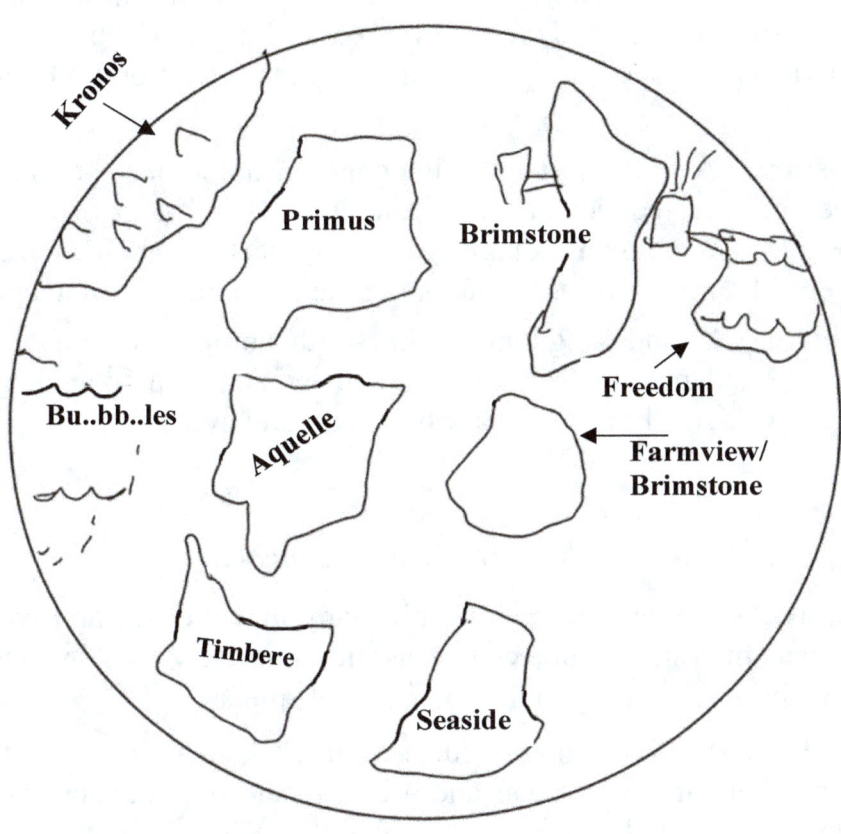

Setting and Geography

Akura…A planet

(On the light side of the planet)

Alteria…The land kingdom which succumbed to the Great Quakes. The remaining land portion is governed by a Council of Elders. Alterians have hazel eyes and blonde hair.

Marinea…The kingdom under the sea formed after the Great Quakes divided the land kingdom of Alteria. Marineans have silver hair and eyes and were governed by kings, now by Queen Tamara. They have retractable gills in order to live on both land and sea.

Mosshire…A land kingdom in the cold north composed of small pieces of forested, ice-covered land joined by bridges, and an impenetrable mountain range. Ruled by Sostor, an ice magic sorcerer. Residents have fair skin, blonde hair and very blue eyes.

Mesarra…A land kingdom in the south composed of a great desert. Residents are from tribes ruled by Sunan, a solar magic mage. Residents have very dark hair, skin and eyes.

*   *   *   *   *

(On the dark side of the planet)

Primus…A verdant kingdom with many greenhouses and well-designed buildings. Subject to seismic activity. Ruled by King Forty, the fortieth king in the sequence of rulers.

Aquelle…A kingdom that includes a huge lake that feeds into the ocean. There are many boats and bridges that offer connections to a series of islands. Previously ruled by King Scimitar; now governed through elections, currently by President Regis.

Timbere…A kingdom situated in a large forest with treehouses linked by aerial pathways. Ruled by Queen Flora III, a Super Sister and Twin to Queen Astrid.

*　　*　　*　　*　　*

Brimstone…A mountainous kingdom with many caves. Previously ruled by King Lucas, a wielder of shadow magic. Now ruled through election by Lucian.

Farmview…A kingdom supplying the kingdom of Brimstone, now part of Brimstone.

Freedom…An island kingdom populated by refugees from Brimstone; ruled by Cyril and his twin brother, Cyrus, both identified as Super Children/Twins.

Seaside…A kingdom on the sea. Ruled by Queen Astrid, a Super Sister and Twin of Queen Flora III.

*　　*　　*　　*　　*

Kronos…A kingdom beneath the mountain range behind Mosshire. Once ruled by King Rupert I, now deceased; presently ruled by King Rupert II, a Super Brother and Twin of Shamous from the kingdom of Marinea and owner of the magical shop **Your Every Wish.** Residents are Elves.

'Bu..bb..les'…A kingdom beneath the 'endless sea' between Kronos and Marinea. Part of both light and dark sides of Akura. Ruled by King Posidon; residents are mermaids and mermen.

*　　*　　*　　*　　*

On another astral plane…

<u>The Crystal Castle</u>

Home of the Super Beings and their Watcher/Guardians.

Elsewhere in the Universe. . .

Starbright...a planet

Starlight... An alien kingdom recently ruled by a King and Queen, killed in a crash of their airship on Akura. Now succeeded by their daughter, **Trixie**, a Super Child living on the planet Akura. If officially crowned Queen, she will be known as **Queen Moonbeam**, after her mother.

Starshine... The second alien kingdom on the planet Starbright. Ruled by Queen Bella, who had been imprisoned by the leaders of a military uprising and is now freed.

*   *   *   *   *

Planet X...a planet

A planet responsible for the unsolved kidnapping of Queen Tamara and Queen-Designate Candace of Marinea. Now threatened by its star going supernova.

Bluegreen...a planet

Planet #1 in the search for a new home suitable for the residents of Planet X.

Cloudy...a planet

Planet #2 in the search for a new home suitable for the residents of Planet X.

Robotic...a planet

Planet #3 in the search for a new home suitable for the residents of Planet X.

Winner...a planet

Planet #4 in the search for a new home suitable for the residents of Planet X.

*   *   *   *   *

Divos...a planet

Location... On the other end of the galaxy; connected to Akura by a Black Hole.

Dubbell... One of two major kingdoms on the planet. Originally ruled by an unnamed Ruler. Populated by pairs of residents: one human and one avatar. Residents wear very colorful clothing.

Thalia... The second major kingdom on the planet. Ruled by Nikos. Residents wear clothing in shades of grey and beige. There is an active Resistance movement.

Communities... Population groups in early stages of political organization.

*   *   *   *   *

Planet G (for Game)...a planet

Location... In another galaxy; elsewhere in the universe. Thought to be seeking more territory.

Cast of Characters (Arranged by Kingdom)

(On the light side of Akura)

<u>Marinea</u>

Tamara…Queen Emerita of Marinea; a Second* Generation Super Child and Sister/Twin to Trina. Married to Sean.

Sean…Commander Emeritus of the Marinean Security Force, Tamara's husband, and a Second* Generation Super Child/Twin to Jon.

Candace (Candy)… New Queen of Marinea; One of four original Super Children of Tamara and Sean. No mirror Twin. Third Generation. Wed to Cyril of Freedom. Mother of Sixth Generation Joy and Twelfth Generation fraternal Twins Fernne and Forrest. Grandmother of Savior (Savvy) and Starr.

Joy…First-born of Candace and Cecil. New Queen-Designate under Candace. Fourth Generation Super Child. Wed to Nolan.

Savvy…First-born of Joy and Nolan. Sixth Generation. Next in line-of-succession to Joy

Sunny…One of four original Super Children of Queen Emerita Tamara and Commander Emeritus Sean. No Mirror Twin. Third Generation. Wed to Cyrus, new Ruler of Freedom. New Queen-Consort to Cyrus.

Skye…One of four original Super Children of Queen Emerita Tamara and Commander Emeritus Sean. No Mirror Twin. Third Generation. Wed to Greta of Marinea. Co-Owner of Pro Bono Shop. Now Space Force Executive Officer under Georgio.

Verd… One of four original Super Children of Queen Emerita Tamara and Commander Emeritus Sean. No Mirror Twin. Third Generation. Wed to Savea of Marinea. Father of Fourth Generation Lavan and Wavan.

Leilani and **Andrea**... Third Generation Super Children/Twin daughters of Queen Emerita Tamara and Commander Emeritus Sean. Leilani is wed to Kert. Andrea is wed to Patrik.

Scarlett and Pepper...The new Twelfth Generation Super Children/fraternal Twins of Queen Emerita Tamara and Commander Emeritus Sean.

*   *   *   *   *

Trina...A Second Generation Super Child and Sister/Twin to Queen Emerita Tamara. Wed to Jon.

Jon...A Second Generation* Super Child/Twin to Commander Emeritus Sean and new commander of the Security Force. Former President of the Academy of Magic. Wed to Trina.

Tristan and **Brendan**...The Third Generation twin sons of Trina and Jon.

*   *   *   *   *

Marigold and **Steele**...Watchers/Nannies to the infant children of Queen Emerita Tamara and Commander Emeritus Sean. New Nannies for Joy.

Pansy and **Cooper**...Watchers/Nannies to the royal children of Trina and Jon.

*   *   *   *   *

Constantine...Tutor to the first-born children of Queen Emerita Tamara and Commander Emeritus Sean. Newly appointed Marinean Historian. Taken into custody by the Marinean Security Force for illegal actions at the Academy of Magic.

Crystos...Former tutor to the twin girls/Super Sisters born to Queen Emerita Tamara and Commander Emeritus Sean. Upgraded to Fourth Generation Super Child and twin to Georgio. Briefly designated Ambassador-Elect to the kingdom of Starshine. Later also a tutor to the foster child, Trixie. Former Second-in-Command of the newly established Space Force. Wed to Trixie.* New President of the Academy of Magic.

* * * * *

Terra…Mother of Queen Emerita Tamara and Trina, wed to Trident; also Head Watcher and non-designated Super Child.

Trident…Father of Queen Emerita Tamara and Trina; wed to Terra; formerly a Prince and King of Marinea; Ambassador to Alteria. Second Generation Twin to Trillium.

Trillium…Trident's Second Generation twin, and Ambassador to Mesarra. Reassigned as Ambassador to Starshine.

Solange… Mother of Trident; Grandmother of Queen Emerita Tamara and Trina; a First Generation Super Child/Twin to Savea. Wed to Sostor. Mother of Coral and Frosti, third Generation Super Sister/Twins/ Children of Solange and Sostor.

* * * * *

Savea…A Third Generation Super Child Sister/Twin to Solange. Wed to Verd*, son of Queen Emerita Tamara and Commander Emeritus Sean. Mother of Lavan and Wavan.

Verd…A first-born Third Generation Super Child of Queen Emerita Tamara and Commander Emeritus Sean, wed to Savea; father of Lavan and Wavan.

Lavan and **Wavan**…Fourth Generation Super Twins/Brothers; children of Savea and Verd.

Daffi and **Bronze**…Watcher/Nannies to the twin sons of Savea and Verd.

* * * * *

Mia…Tamara's personal attendant.

Dr. Astarte…Royal Physician to the royal court.

Amanda…Tamara's Social Secretary.

* * * * *

Georgio…Experienced member of the Security Force and tutoring assistant to Constantine in service to the royal children in the Crystal Castle. Once the children became adults, he was appointed as interim Ambassador to Mosshire and interim manager of the Academy President's office. He has completed Graduate Studies at the Academy and finished his doctoral research. Fourth Generation Super Child and twin to Crystos. Wed to Rose*. Appointed Commander of the new Space Force.

*　　*　　*　　*　　*

Merlynn…Faux Admissions Officer avatar at the Academy of Magic on Marinea (and former Queen Consort to King Scimitar).

Shamous…Owner of **Your Every Wish**, a magical shop on Marinea. Crown Prince of Kronos, a Super Child/Twin of Rupert II.

Greta…Co-Owner of Pro Bono shop, and a Third Generation* Super Child/Twin to Moonstone. Wed to Skye.

Vera…New Pro Bono lawyer in charge of interns.

Professor Yexer…Dissident at the Academy of Magic.

Trixie…Ringleader of older female magic students who 'acted out' at the Palace. Newly-discovered Queen-Designate of the kingdom of **Starlight** and Fourth Generation* Super Child. Super twin to Arkin. Now Recruitment Manager of the Space Force. Wed to Crystos.

Arkin…Newly-identified First Generation Super Child and Marinean Ambassador Designate to Starlight. Super fraternal twin to Trixie.

Moonstone…Newly-identified First Generation Super Child and Twin to Greta. New Marinean Ambassador to Starlight.

Stefan…Fellow Graduate student and love interest of Andrea. Ambassador to Marinea from Planet X.

Dr. Hanover…Special Scientific Consultant to the Crown.

Marinean Security Force

Sean…Commander Emeritus.

Jon…New Commander.

Dana…Second-in-Command.

Jon and Borel…Members of the Marinean Security Force's Special Task Force.

Mimi and Clark…New members of the Security Task Force.

Franc and Kari…Members of the Force selected to work with the twins to redesign the Practice Sessions.

Alteria

Trident…Father of Tamara and Trina; wed to Terra; formerly a prince and King of Marinea; Second Generation Super Child; Marinean Ambassador to Alteria.

Terra…Mother of Queen Emerita Tamara and Trina; wed to Trident; also Head Watcher; undesignated Super Child.

Tomas…Executive Assistant to Trident. Non-Magical Co-Leader of 'New Friends.'

Mimi…Magical co-leader of 'New Friends.'

Fern…A realtor from Alteria and friend of Terra.

Rose…Daughter of Queen Flora III of Timbere and Ambassador from Timbere to Alteria. Fourth* Generation Super Child/Twin to Merlynn. Wed to Georgio.

Violet…Executive Assistant to Rose.

New Space Force

(based on Alteria)

Georgio…Commander.

Skye… Second-in-Command.

Klyde…One of two original Communicators in Georgio's office. Transferred to the Academy President's Office to work with Crystos.

Preme…One of two original Communicators in Georgio's office. Assigned to Georgio.

Trixie…Head of Recruitment.

Leilani…One of two original staff members in Trixie's office. Transferred to Skye's service.

Andrea…Trixie's original staff.

Kert…Captain of Explorer 1.

Nolan…Captain of Explorer 2, then Explorer 4.

Joy…Captain of Explorer 3.

Dr. Jeen…Medical Doctor on Explorer 3.

Mosshire

Sostor…An ice magic sorcerer on Mosshire; Ruler of the kingdom; a First Generation Super Child/Twin to Sunan of Mesarra; has fair skin, blonde hair and very blue eyes like residents of Mosshire. Wed to Solange, a Super Child/Sister to Savea.

Solange…Mother of Trident and Trillium; Grandmother of Tamara and Trina; a First Generation Super Child/Twin to Savea. Wed to Sostor.

Coral and **Frosti**…Second Generation Super Sister/Twins/ Children of Solange and Sostor.

Pansy and Chrome…Watcher/Nannies to the twin girls of Solange and Sostor.

*   *   *   *   *

Rolf…Watcher and temporary ruler of Mosshire; and leader of an insurrection.

Trina…A Second Generation Super Child and Sister/Twin to Queen Emerita Tamara. Wed to Jon. Former Marinean Ambassador to Mosshire.

Georgio…Interim Marinean Ambassador to Mosshire. (see Marinea for more complete description).

Mesarra

Sunan…A solar magic mage on Mesarra; Ruler of the kingdom; a First Generation Super Child/Twin to Sostor of Mosshire; has dark hair and eyes like residents of Mesarra. Wed to Merlynn.

Merlynn…Sunan's Assistant in establishing an Academy of Magic in Mesarra. A First Generation Super Child and Sister/Twin to Rose. Offered the position of Ambassador from Marinea to Mesarra by Queen Tamara. Wed to Sunan.

Trillium…A Second Generation Super Child/Twin to Trident and Trident's identical twin; Marinean Ambassador to Mesarra. Reassigned as Marinean Ambassador to Starshine. Wed to Delia.

Delia…Trillium's first hire, the Embassy Manager on Mesarra. A First Generation Super Child, upgraded to Second Generation*. Wed to Trillium.

Carter…Delia's new Assistant.

Claud…Brief Prime Minister of Mesarra.

(On the dark side of Akura)

Primus

Forty…King of the kingdom of Primus (Personal name: **Linc**).

Martine…Member of Marinean Security Force; Marinean Ambassador to Primus.

Viktor…Commander-Designate of the new Seismic Alert Guard.

Aquelle

Scimitar…Former King of the kingdom of Aquelle; masqueraded as a rogue Watcher; sidekick of King Lucas of Brimstone. Now deceased.

Regis…Present Ruler and former Prime Minister of Aquelle.

Borel…Member of the Marinean Security Force; Marinean Ambassador to Aquelle.

Anna…Tour guide on Aquelle and first Executive Assistant to Borel.

Pieter…Second Executive Assistant to Borel.

Timbere

Flora III…Queen of the kingdom of Timbere; a First Generation Super Child and Sister/Twin to Queen Astrid of Seaside.

Rose…Daughter of Queen Flora III; a Second Generation Super Child/Twin to Merlynn. Timberean Ambassador to Alteria. Wed to Georgio*.

Brooke…Secretary to Queen Flora.

Talia…Member of Marinean Security Force; Marinean Ambassador to Timbere.

Hazel…Executive Assistant to Talia.

Clark…Magical Co-Leader of the new experimental project in Timbere. Also a member of the Marinean Security Force. Temporary Ambassador to Alteria.

Borys…Non-magical Co-Leader of the new experimental project in Timbere.

Acorn… Owner of the tree-top restaurant.

Brimstone

Lucas…Former King of the kingdom of Brimstone. Wielder of shadow magic. Now deceased.

Lucian…Former government official and elected Ruler.

Scimitar…Former King of the kingdom of Aquelle; masqueraded as a rogue Watcher; sidekick of King Lucas. Now deceased.

Merlynn…True Admissions Officer of the Academy of Magic on Marinea; First Generation Super Child and Sister/Twin to Rose. Declared Queen Consort to King Scimitar at one point. The majority of her life was spent in captivity in Brimstone. Now helping Sunan establish an Academy of Magic in Mesarra. Granted Marinean citizenship by Queen Tamara and appointed as Marinean Ambassador to Mesarra. Wed to Sunan.

Exeter…Marinean Ambassador to Brimstone.

Angus…Once Ambassador-Designate to Farmview. Now Deputy Ambassador to Brimstone.

Freedom

(Name of the new island kingdom east of Brimstone, populated by refugees from Brimstone)

Cyril…Former Ruler of the kingdom and Super Child/Twin brother of Cyrus. Wed to Queen Candace of Marinea and Consort to the Queen.

Cyrus…New Ruler of the kingdom. Super Child/Twin brother of Cyril and former Second-in-Command. Wed to Sunny of Marinea.

Seaside

Astrid…Queen of the kingdom of Seaside; a First Generation Super Child and Sister/Twin of Queen Flora III of Timbere.

Kalia…Member of Marinean Security Force; Marinean Ambassador to Seaside.

Margo…Kalia's guide in Seaside.

Kronos

Rupert I…King of the Elven kingdom of Kronos, now deceased.

Rupert II…Present King of the Elven kingdom of Kronos, a First Generation Super Child/Twin of Shamous from Marinea.

Shamous…New Crown Prince of Kronos, a First Generation Super Child/Twin of Rupert II. Owner of **Your Every Wish**, a magical shop in Marinea.

Damon…Soldier and Tour Guide.

'Bu..bb..les'

Posidon…King of the undersea kingdom of 'Bu..bb..les.'

Shelley One…Daughter of King Posidon, a First Generation Super Child and Sister/Twin of Shelley Two.

Shelley Two…Daughter of King Posidon, a First Generation Super Child and Sister/Twin of Shelley One.

Dani…Marinean Ambassador to Bu..bb..les.

(On another astral plane)

The Crystal Castle

Adele and **Jeremy**…The Emeritus Super Beings.

Tamara and **Sean**…New Super Beings.

Elsa…Watcher/Guardian at the Crystal Castle.

Rogere…Watcher/Guardian at the Crystal Castle; Trident's and Trillium's biological father.

Bugle…Temporary Head Watcher.

(Elsewhere in the Universe)

Starlight

An alien kingdom on the planet **Starbright.** Recently ruled by a King and Queen who were killed in a crash of their airship on Akura. Now succeeded by their daughter, **Trixie,** a Super Child living on the planet Akura.

Skort…Prime Minister of Starlight.

Arkin…Marinean Ambassador-Designate to Starlight; Super fraternal Twin to Trixie.

Beamie…Guide on Starlight who helped Arkin establish his Embassy.

Moonstone…New Marinean Ambassador to Starlight; First Generation Super Twin to Greta.

Neero…Leader of the Insurrectionists.

Shine…Embassy Chief-of-Staff.

Scotti…Manager of the Marinean Embassy Residence.

Trone…Leader of the Starlight Resistance.

Starshine

Another kingdom on the planet **Starbright.** (once known as Starlight). Ruled by Queen Bella, who had previously been imprisoned by the leaders of a military uprising and is now freed.

Bella…Queen of Starshine.

Malkum…Consort of the Queen.

Crystos…Originally appointed Marinean Ambassador to Starshine but reassigned as Second-in-Command of the Space Force. Now President of the Academy of Magic in Marinea. First Generation Super Child and Twin to Georgio. Upgraded by the Creator Being to a Fourth Generation being.

Former Planet X

(Now temporarily named 'Winner')

The Ruler…As yet unnamed.

Stefan…Ambassador from Planet X to Marinea.

Jaeda…Ambassador from Marinea to Planet X.

Thalia

A kingdom on the planet Divos on the other side of the galaxy. There is an active Resistance movement.

Nikos…the Ruler.

Kert…a refugee from Thalia who escaped through a Black Hole and reached Akura. Identified as a Super Child. Patrik's fraternal twin brother.

Patrik…a refugee from Thalia who escaped through a Black Hole and reached Akura. Identified as a Super Child. Kert's fraternal twin brother.

Dubbell

A kingdom on the planet Divos on the other side of the universe. Human residents are paired with avatars.

Ruler unnamed…Incarcerated by Security Force.

Unknown Planet G

Nolan… an alien who entered a Black Hole located on the far side of the universe reaching Akura via the arc of Time.

First Generation Super Children Twins
(and their home kingdoms)

<u>Female</u>

Solange (Marinea/Mosshire) and **Savea** (Marinea)

Astrid (Seaside) and **Flora** (Timbere)

Rose (Timbere) and **Merlynn** (Brimstone/Marinea)

Shelley One and **Shelley Two** (Bu..bb..les)

Trixie (Marinea/Starlight) and **Arkin** (male, Marinea/ Starlight)

Greta (Marinea) and **Moonstone** (Marinea and Starlight)

<u>Male</u>

Sostor (Mosshire) and **Sunan** (Mesarra)

Rupert II (Kronos) and **Shamous** (Marinea/Kronos)

Arkin (Marinea/Starlight) and **Trixie** (female, Marinea/ Starlight)

Georgio (Marinea) and **Crystos** (Marinea)

Second Generation Super Children
<u>(Marinea)</u>

Tamara (Alteria/Marinea) and **Trina** (Alteria/Marinea)

Trident (Marinea) and **Trillium** (Marinea)

<u>(Mosshire)</u>

Coral and **Frosti**…Second Generation Super Sisters Twins/Children of Solange and Sostor.

Third Generation Super Children
(Marinea)

Candace...Queen of Marinea and Daughter of Queen Emerita Tamara and Commander Emeritus Sean. An original Super Child. Wed to Cyril.

Skye...Prince and Son of Queen Emerita Tamara and Commander Emeritus Sean. An original Super Child. Wed to Greta.

Sunny...Princes and daughter of Queen Emerita Tamara and Commander Emeritus Sean. An original Super Child. Wed to Cyrus.

Verd...Prince and Son of Queen Emerita Tamara and Commander Emeritus Sean. An original Super Child. Wed to Savea; father of Lavan and Wavan.

Cyril...Upgraded after being wed to Candace.

Tristan and **Brendan**...the twin sons of Trina and Jon.

Fourth Generation Super Children
(Marinea)

Lavan and **Wavan**...Super Twins/Brothers; children of Savea and Verd.

Leilani and **Andrea**...the twin daughters of Tamara and Sean.

Crystos. . . Upgraded to Fourth Generation by the Creator Being.

Sixth Generation Super Children
(Marinea/Freedom)

Joy...First-born daughter of Candace and Cyril. New Queen-Designate.

Nolan...Upgraded by Creator Being.

Eighth Generation Super Children (Marinea)

Savior (Savvy)...First-born of Joy and Nolan

Tenth Generation Super Children (Marinea)

Starr. . .Second-born of Joy and Nolan

Twelfth Generation Super Children (Marinea)

Scarlett and Pepper...New fraternal twins of Queen Emerita Tamara and Commander Emeritus Sean Lockette

Fernne and **Forrest**...New fraternal twins of Queen Candace and Consort Cecil.

---

*The Creator Being has a policy of upgrading so that both wedded parties are the same generation.

Other updates are now evident – new information has surfaced via a spell that assigns accurate Generational status. Some of the prior assumptions have been superseded.

Crystal Saga Series 4

3 — The New Order

D. E. Weingand

Prologue

My name is Candace. I am one of the four first-born children of Queen Tamara and Commander Sean. When the order of succession was established, I was named Queen-Designate and I have served in that role several times when my mother was deemed unavailable.

My world has just been turned upside down. Since my mother has been such an exemplary Queen and is still in good health, I expected that I would not be called upon to become Queen for a long time. However, that proved to be a false assumption.

Apparently, the Creator Being's Grand Design calls for the retirement of the two present Super Beings and the appointment of two new ones. The present Super Beings, Adele and Jeremy, have served in those positions for a long time, but they have been focused on themselves—which is no longer a viable approach in today's expanding universe.

The two new Super Beings selected are my parents…and they were totally unaware of this imminent change. Fortunately, there were existing rules of succession for both of them—but that didn't lessen the shock of sudden and unexpected change in their lives.

I totally empathize, since I was unprepared as well. I am pleased, of course, that the talents and experience of my parents have been recognized, but I deeply sympathize with the trauma that they are going through.

However, I knew that this day would come at some point in my life; I'm just struggling with the suddenness of its arrival. My mate, Cecil, is also deeply affected. He is the Ruler of the kingdom of Freedom…and has pledged to me from the beginning of our relationship that he would turn that role over to his twin brother Cyrus when I became Queen. He, too, must deal with that long-ago promise.

And then there's my sister, Sunny. She is wed to Cyrus. So when he takes over as Ruler of Freedom, she will have responsibilities there, which will require her to cut back on her passion for producing, directing, and starring in the theater.

So many of my loved ones will be affected, not just me. Therefore, I've decided to do my duty, of course. But also, I intend to infringe as little as possible on the lives of other family members. I know what can happen with good intentions, but I'm going to try.

Finally, I know my children's and grandchildren's lives will be impacted as well. But I worry less about them—which sounds strange, I know. But Joy and Savvy are so powerful in their own right—and determined to chart their own paths—that I am certain they will handle this well.

So a grand adventure lies ahead. I'm sure there will be ups and downs, but I've faced them before. Wish me well.

Chapter 1
The First Night

Tamara opened her eyes in the Crystal Castle. She was relieved to see Sean beside her. "What happened?" she asked.

Sean hugged her and replied, "Your emotions took over, my Dear. I think the Castle stepped in to give us both a break. Our family members at dinner have a lot to process, as well. It's probably good to take a step back."

Looking around, Tamara noticed that they were in the chamber where they had spent their honeymoon. "Do you think this is going to be our bedroom now?" she wondered. A knock at the door admitted Elsa and Rogere.

"I see that the Castle thinks you need some peace and quiet," Elsa began. "You will find that the Castle has opinions, but you'll get used to it!"

Sean laughed, "I knew that the two of you have duties here, but I didn't know the Castle was sentient! Is there a way to be proactive and communicate with it directly, or do we just react?"

Rogere smiled, "We'll give you a tutorial in Castle 101, but not today. We understand how overwhelmed you must be, and we've ordered dinner to be brought here to your quarters."

Elsa added, "Tamara, you are correct that this was the room in which you spent your honeymoon. However, you will find that your quarters are now actually much larger, containing several more rooms. Should you need anything changed, you have only to ask the Castle to do so."

"Really?" inquired Tamara. "How fascinating! When do we start our tutorial?"

"Tomorrow morning, you can ask the Castle to return you to Akura," advised Rogere. "Once you get everything stabilized there and the Coronation of Candace is accomplished, you can ask the Castle to bring you back here and we can begin your indoctrination."

"How do we do that?" asked Sean.

"Just send a mental message," answered Elsa. "The Castle will hear you. It is an extension of the Creator Being. Tamara, your mother is very familiar with how it operates and she will be accessible to you as well."

Relieved, Tamara relaxed. "So if I call, she will come?"

"Absolutely," assured Rogere. "Now, if you will excuse me, I will see to your dinner." He vanished.

"Elsa, we just finished dinner," complained Tamara.

"You forget that Time is different here," reminded Elsa. "Your bodies are already hungry."

2

A rumbling in their tummies supported that statement as Elsa produced a table set for dinner and two chairs.

"Won't you join us for dinner?" asked Tamara.

"Another time," replied Elsa. "This is your first night here and we are respecting your privacy." Then she vanished.

Tamara and Sean walked over to a window and gazed at the clouds while they waited for dinner to arrive.

*   *   *   *   *

Tamara was surprised how well she slept in the Castle. Sean had a similar experience. When breakfast arrived the next morning, they were hungry again and ate with gusto. Soon they heard a knock at the door; Rogere and Elsa entered when invited.

"Did you have a good first night?" asked Elsa.

"I slept very well," admitted Tamara, "but I couldn't find a shower this morning."

"That will be part of your Castle 101 tutorial," said Rogere. "Today, the Castle cleansed you while you were sleeping. Your clothes were also made fit for another day. Are you ready to return to Akura?"

"You'll notice that he doesn't say 'home' because this is your home now," added Elsa. "However, we recognize that you have plans to initiate on Akura to set the New Order in motion."

"I should warn you that you will arrive at the precise moment you left," warned Elsa. "That is why you weren't given a change of clothing."

"Before we go," Tamara began, "I need to ask you something. I looked in a mirror when I awoke and my pendant had changed again. Can you explain that?"

Sean reached other his shirt and looked at his pendant—which also looked different. Both pendants now had a ring of clear crystals beyond the rainbow ring.

Rogere and Elsa looked at both pendants and Elsa speculated, "It may be a special designation of your new roles. We will have to ask the Creator Being."

"We will now give you the transit instructions," began Rogere. "When you are ready to return, just reverse them."

Elsa said, "Hold hands and think about the last thing you did on Akura at the party. I believe you were strolling around the dining room, chatting with family members. To return here, hold hands again and visualize this room."

Tamara and Sean followed their instructions and…

Suddenly they were strolling through the dining room, smiling and talking to family. Sean squeezed Tamara's hand as they continued to move through their guests. Sean extended his hand and invited her to dance. As they twirled around to the music, he whispered, "Our new adventure has begun. What do we do first?"

Tamara thought for a moment and said, "We plan the Coronation—right after we have a heart-to-heart meeting with all affected parties. I want to make this transition as smooth as possible for them."

"I agree," responded Sean. "After the Coronation, I will activate the succession model on my side of this process. But until then, we must focus on Candace."

"I've been watching her," commented Tamara. "She obviously has hidden acting talent. No one would ever guess that her life has just been upended.

"I'm going to send out a mental message to the key players in this first drama inviting them to breakfast here tomorrow. Then we will discuss the New Order."

Her message went out to Candace, Sunny, Joy and their mates. Tamara knew it had been received, as each of them stiffened before nodding to her. The New Order had been set in motion.

Chapter 2
Coronation Planning

The next morning, Tamara and Sean arrived at the Private Dining Room early. Candace and Cecil were the first to join them. They looked tired, ascribing it to staying up late at the party. But Tamara knew that change was weighing heavily on them.

She hugged her daughter tightly; Sean ignored Cecil's outstretched hand and hugged him as well. Everyone had tears in their eyes.

Next to arrive was Sunny, together with Cyrus, closely followed by Joy and Nolan. Three unexpected family members entered last: Terra, Savvy and Starr.

Terra informed everyone that the Creator Being had charged her with being a liaison during the preparation for the Coronation. Savvy and Starr showed up just because they wanted to!

*   *   *   *   *

After the breakfast had satisfied everyone's hunger, it was time to address any questions that might be present. Tamara was glad that her mother had joined them as a liaison. She would be very helpful.

Candace decided to speak first. She looked at Cyril and asked an important question. "Are you still offering to trade positions with Cyrus once I am proclaimed Queen?"

"I am a man of my word, Dear," he reminded her. "I intend to support you in every way that I can. I will also be available to Cyrus if he wishes. I have complete faith that he will do an excellent job as Ruler of Freedom.

"We can acquire an apartment in Freedom for when either of us needs to be there, but I will give the keys to the Executive Residence to Cyrus. Obviously, our primary home will be here in Marinea."

Candace smiled and thanked him for his generous spirit. Then she looked at Cyrus and Sunny. "How can I be of assistance to you in this transition?" she asked.

Sunny looked thoughtful, "I've been thinking about that. It's almost time to start recruiting for a third play. I plan to produce and direct it in Freedom. Other locations will have to welcome the touring companies.

"I'm confident that having Freedom as the main production site will make it possible to fulfill my duties as the mate of the Ruler. Cyrus, do you see any problems?"

Cyrus shook his head and thanked her for her careful consideration of what would be required of her.

Terra spoke next, "I'm impressed that so much thought has already been given to the requirements of this New Order. I will be available to all of you…just ask."

Candace turned to her daughter, "Joy, I know you want to continue as Captain in the Space Force. Have you considered what you would do if you were needed to step in as Queen—as I have done for Mama in the past?"

At this point, Tamara interrupted, saying, "I named this change 'The New Order' and I am prepared to consider new approaches to making it work. Although Joy will be the Queen-Designate in the line of succession, as Queen Emerita I could be tapped to step in for you as needed. This has never been done before, but I see no reason why it could not be done successfully."

Joy moved to give Tamara a hug, "Thank you, Grandma. I think that's a brilliant idea!"

Starr had been listening quietly, but now he commented, "I have analyzed that model for the future and it will be very effective. I approve."

Tamara nodded and asked, "It seems that our planning can move on to the Coronation itself, unless there are other questions or concerns." Hearing none, she ordered some refreshments and shifted the conversation to the Coronation.

*   *   *   *   *

As Tamara began asking Candace about her preferences for the ceremony, there was a flash of light and Shamous appeared.

"I am at your service in this time of need," he offered. "As you know, I have a great deal of experience in wedding planning. This ceremony will be on a grander scale, but I am up to the challenge."

Candace stood and moved to hug him. "Just having you here takes a lot of stress away from me," she exclaimed. "I'm so glad to see you!"

Shamous flushed, but returned the hug. "I am here for you. We will make this a very special day, even though it is a sudden and unexpected occasion. Don't fret, my dear. Everything will be fine."

Candace sighed and felt herself relax. Now that Shamous was involved, she knew that he spoke the truth.

*   *   *   *   *

Tamara was not surprised that Shamous took over the planning of the Coronation. She smiled as she watched her family fall under his influence, enjoying themselves in the process. She could leave everything in his capable hands. It was time to turn her attention to the Security Force.

Chapter 3
Security Force 2.0

Tamara had issued another breakfast invitation for the next day. On the guest list were Jon and Trina, Georgio and Crystos, Trixie, Dana, Leilani and Andrea. As Liaison, Terra was expected to attend as well.

Once again, Tamara and Sean arrived early in order to greet their guests personally. This group of guests had not as yet been briefed on the New Order and its potential consequences.

After everyone had arrived and was seated, Tamara asked her mother to summarize the events that had occurred and then open the meeting to questions and comments. She was not surprised to see flashes of shock and disbelief on their faces.

When calm had been restored, Tamara waved the servers in and suggested that the meeting would continue after breakfast. Sean whispered to her that appetites may have been affected by the news. She nodded and turned on some relaxing music.

When Tamara restarted the meeting, she asked Sean to summarize the contents of the Security Force's Rules of Succession. As he did so, he stressed that the Rules had not been updated since written. Therefore, Jon was listed as Second-in-Command, rather than Dana.

Apologizing to Dana for the oversight, Sean asked him if he would be willing to chair a committee to update the Rules. Dana nodded his understanding and agreed to do so.

Sean then continued his presentation by asking Jon and Dana to meet with him in his office, which was nearby, while the rest of the guests enjoyed a short break. The three men left the dining room.

In Sean's office, they sat around a small table and Sean opened a bottle of bubbly. "I didn't realize until this morning when I looked for a copy of the Rules of Succession that there would be a problem," he admitted. "Please let me know your feelings honestly."

The three men had worked together for so long and with good will, there was no hesitancy in talking frankly. Dana spoke first, "I have no problem with Jon taking over. He is a very experienced and capable leader. I would be proud to be Second-in-Command to him, provided he is willing to resign the Presidency of the Academy."

"I guess I'm next," said Jon. "I have enjoyed my time at the Academy, but I also think that new blood would be good for the institution. I thank Dana for his kind words and would welcome him as my Second-in-Command."

"I applaud your honest responses and thank you for them," Sean said. "In this transition period, every time a vacancy occurs and someone is appointed to fill it, another vacancy emerges.

"Jon, what do you think about asking Crystos to assume the Presidency? He has a distinguished background in education," Sean inquired.

"That's an excellent suggestion," Jon replied. "And then the Space Force vacancy will need to be addressed."

"Exactly what I was saying," laughed Sean. "Shall we return to the Dining Room?"

*   *   *   *   *

Back in the Dining Room, Sean reported the results of his meeting with Jon and Dana. Sounds of 'Congratulations!' resounded around the room. Crystos and Georgio began to hold a private mental communication.

As they looked up, Crystos stood and said, "After consulting with Commander Georgio, I accept the office of Presidency of the Academy."

Georgio then stood, stating, "Crystos will be an excellent President. I request an opportunity to discuss the path forward with my staff, all of whom are present. We will let you know what we decide as soon as possible. This is a classic example of the game of Dominos!"

Sean laughed, "Just what we were saying in our brief meeting. It's a difficult time for all of us. Tamara and I were totally blindsided by the Creator Being and will do our best to make the transition as smooth as possible."

Everyone then stood and showed their appreciation for the leadership shown by Tamara and Sean. Terra joined in the applause. She was proud of her daughter and son-in-law. They will be true assets in the Crystal Castle.

*   *   *   *   *

Georgio asked his staff to come with him to a secure conference room across from the Private Dining Room. Once seated, he complimented them on their service to the Space Force and emphasized that his door would always be open to them.

He continued, "I would like to meet with each of you tomorrow morning. Please use the time until then to think about your future hopes as well as your present positions.

"I would like to hear your thoughts and then I will make

some staffing adjustments that I hope will be appreciated," he concluded.

*   *   *   *   *

As the meeting ended, Jon was watching Trina's face. They had been so happy working together in the President's office. He knew that his decision was not setting well with her, and he wished they could have discussed it. He had some relationship repair ahead.

Moving toward her, he kissed her cheek and suggested a walk in the Garden. She smiled up at him with tears in her eyes and they left the room.

It didn't take long to find a vacant bench. They claimed it and began to talk. He started with an apology and asked for her patience and understanding. Holding her close, he tried to make her aware of how precipitously everyone at the breakfast meeting would need to react and reorganize their lives.

As her eyes overflowed with tears, he hugged her. "I know you are aware that I have been thinking of leaving the Academy," he began. "I also realize that you were relieved when you thought I was no longer in danger by working in the Security Force. What you may not have known is that my heart was always still in the Force. The safety of our kingdom is always top-of-mind for me."

Trina nodded that she did understand; she was just scared. "Your willingness to return to the Force is no surprise to me. I just wish I had been consulted."

Jon kissed her, saying, "I know. I wish that, too. But events have caught up with all of us. I suspect Tamara has shed her share of tears as well."

A flash of light and Terra was with them. Sitting on the other side of Trina, she held Trina's hand and let a calming spell surround her. "Jon is right about the nature of these developments," she said. "Sean needed an immediate answer…and your sister has shed a lot of tears.

"I have been appointed as liaison for this transition; I am here for you whenever you need me," she stressed.

"Mother, you are always available, that's not new!" laughed Trina through her tears.

"Just know you are not alone in this adjustment," added Terra. "And I think you will enjoy working with Crystos. He has a good heart."

Jon suggested, "I have an idea. Let's go to our place and we'll order some take-out. We can try and find some silver linings in these dark clouds!"

"I'll bet the boys will want pizza!" predicted Trina.

Laughing, the three of them teleported out of the Garden.

Chapter 4
Space Force 2.0

Georgio's staff appeared right on time; he was pleased. He had also invited a guest: Starr. Starr had asked to be included, and Georgio had no reason to deny his request. The young man should still be an infant, but Joy had advanced her personal growth—and her children had made even greater strides in their own rates of development.

Even more remarkable were the advanced Generations they represented: Joy was a 6, Savvy was an 8…and Starr was a 10! With each advancement was a boost in power and abilities. There was no doubt that all of them were assets to the Space Force.

Joy was already the Captain of Explorer 3. Nolan, her mate, had been her Executive Officer while his new Ship, Explorer 4, was being completed. That had now happened, so Joy and Nolan each needed a Second-in-Command.

Both Savvy and Starr were ideal candidates. Their rapid growth and Generation status had allowed them to attend and graduate from the Academy in record time.

Georgio had asked his staff to think about their hopes and dreams for advancement in the Force. He hoped that they had done that. When he started this meeting, he had asked them to share, without prejudice, what conclusions they had reached.

The three Explorer Captains—Kert, Joy and Nolan— shared that they were exactly where they should be at this time. Since Explorers 5 and 6 were presently under construction, future advancement was possible. There were some vacancies in the crews of the three Ships that needed to be filled, however.

In terms of recruitment, Trixie and twins Leilani and Andrea expressed satisfaction with their roles at this point in their careers. In the future, they intended to dream more broadly, but not now.

That left Savvy and Starr as two wild cards, eager to be plugged into permanent positions in the Force. Georgio had struggled with ideas —including his own Second-in-Command slot, which had been vacated when Crystos took over the Presidency of the Academy—but he had not reached any decisions as yet. While there was no doubt that both siblings were very talented, they would need more training before taking over positions of major responsibility. Savvy had the most experience; Starr was literally a 'star' of the future! Both Explorers 3 and 4 were in need of Executive Officers... that might be an ideal posting for Joy's two children. It would be a good training experience.

Georgio's mind turned to his vacancy. Then he had a great idea! Skye is a lawyer. His work with Greta in the Pro Bono Shop had been outstanding. Georgio wondered if Skye would be interested—and able—to keep that going while also serving as his Second-in-Command. His lawyer mind would be a tremendous asset to this office. He would ask.

His thoughts had been drifting. He should apologize to his staff…and also share the conclusions that he had reached. Hoping that everyone would be on board, he began to speak.

*   *   *   *   *

Georgio was relieved. His staff had been very supportive of his decisions. His only omission had been Skye. He needed to pursue that idea with Skye in person. When he dismissed his staff, he teleported to the Pro Bono Shop.

Entering the Shop, Georgio looked around, but couldn't locate Skye. He did see Greta and walked over to her. She was working at a desk in the open area. Glancing up, she saw him and rose to give him a hug.

"How nice of you to visit," she said. "How can I help you?"

Georgio admitted that he was looking for Skye, but commented that it was good to see her. She took his arm and led him over to Skye's private office.

"I don't think he's with a client, so you can go right in," Greta assured him.

Knocking at the door and hearing "Enter", Georgio went inside. "Georgio!" exclaimed Skye, "What a surprise! Please sit down."

Georgio obeyed and began to carefully introduce his reason for coming. Skye leaned back in his chair, listening. His face didn't divulge any reaction to what he was hearing. When Georgio had completed his argument, Skye thanked him for the offer—but emphasized his commitment to the Pro Bono Shop.

A soft knock at the door and Greta joined them. Taking a seat, she reminded Skye that Change was a new constant in all their lives. She asked Skye and Georgio to consider whether there was any way to restructure his schedule to somehow accommodate both responsibilities.

Both men looked thoughtful. Georgio hoped that Skye was still considering his offer.

Before they could respond, Greta added, "I have been approached by the Academy asking whether we could start an internship program for some of their law students. I haven't as yet responded to the request. Could that take up some of the slack, Skye?"

Skye's eyes began to gleam as he digested that new information. "Are you willing to oversee such a new endeavor, Greta?" he asked.

Greta nodded. "I think it has real promise for both the Academy and our Shop."

Skye stood and extended his hand to Georgio. "If you can find the necessary flexibility on your end, Georgio, I would be interested in pursuing it on a trial basis."

Georgio smiled and shook his hand. "I'm sure we can make it work, Skye. When can you start?"

"As soon as Greta has the internship program up and running," promised Skye.

Thanking Greta for her creative input, Georgio invited both of them to join him at the local pub. Since no clients were waiting for attention, Skye and Greta agreed to close up early and accept Georgio's invitation.

Walking to the pub, they chatted amiably. A new and different future lay just ahead.

Chapter 5
New Assignments

With Greta's help, Skye was able to efficiently rearrange his schedule. He was pleased to observe her excitement about working with Academy student interns. She was convinced that the interns would enter their professional lives with a new appreciation of pro bono work.

Two weeks later, he found himself knocking at Georgio's office door. It was his first day in the Space Force's Administrative Wing. Entering, he took a seat opposite Georgio, waiting for an orientation to begin.

Skye was startled when Georgio opened his mind and a flood of intel washed over him.

"Wow!" he exclaimed, "That was intense! I've never absorbed intel that way before."

"I find it a good way to efficiently bring staff up to speed," Georgio smiled. "Now, come with me and we'll go to your new office."

Leaving his office, Georgio turned to the right. Passing an open door, he stopped and introduced Skye to two Space Force staff. "These are our Communicators," explained Georgio. "They keep our schedules, take dictation, and other duties as assigned. Their names are Klyde and Preme. Preme works directly for me; Klyde will handle your needs."

Moving on, they stopped at the next door. The door was already labeled with Skye's name and title: 'Executive Officer'. Georgio commented, "I prefer that title to 'Assistant or the like. It is the same as the title given to Second-in-Command staff on our Ships. By virtue of that title, you automatically are placed next in our Order of Succession, should anything happen to me. Crystos held that position before leaving to assume the post of President of the Academy."

Stunned, Skye stammered, "I didn't realize the ramifications of agreeing to join your staff, Sir. I am both honored and surprised. I will do my best to deserve your trust."

They entered Skye's office and Skye noted that there were connecting doors into the office of the Communicators and Georgio's office. It was an efficient arrangement. On a sideboard, a bottle of bubbly stood with four glasses. Georgio called the Communicators to join them and they raised their glasses to toast the new member of the team.

*   *   *   *   *

When Skye arrived home that evening, Greta was eagerly waiting for intel about his new position. But even she was astonished at the level of responsibility and authority he would be assuming.

"I admit to being overwhelmed, Greta." he sighed. "I worry that if I give this position my proper attention, I will inevitably shortchange the Pro Bono Shop."

"I understand, my Dear," Greta agreed. "I expected that you would feel this way. We are co-owners of the Shop, so your office will remain to use whenever you can be there. Clearly, your new duties have to take priority.

"How do you feel about hiring another lawyer to supervise the interns and take over new clients?" she asked.

Skye grimaced and sadly nodded that such an arrangement might be necessary. "Let's hire a contractor to create two more private offices and a third large one for the interns," advised Skye. "My Space Force salary can easily fund that expenditure."

"That's a great idea," smiled Greta. "The Shop's open space can easily accommodate your ideas. By the way, the Universe must be listening to us because a newly-graduated lawyer came in today looking for a permanent position. She was very impressive; I liked her."

"Hmm," sighed Skye, "I leave and our Pro Bono effort expands. I'm not sure I like the sound of that!"

Greta laughed, "Don't let your ego get in your way, my Dear. These changes feel right to me."

* * * * *

The next day, Georgio walked into Skye's office to deliver some sad news: Klyde, Skye's Communicator, had requested a transfer to Crystos' new office at the Academy. They had worked together so well that he wished to continue the relationship.

Skye nodded, saying, "I'm not surprised. That often happens when personnel changes occur. Could we talk to Trixie about the present demands of her Recruiting efforts? Perhaps one of the twins would like to fill in here?"

"Funny you should mention that," laughed Georgio. "She was just asking to come in and discuss that very thing. Can you meet with us in an hour?"

"Absolutely," agreed Skye. "Will the twins be part of the discussion?"

"I believe so," replied Georgio, and he returned to his office.

* * * * *

Skye was happy to be able to reconnect with his twin sisters. It had been some time since he had been able to do so.. His work at the Pro Bono Shop had been all-consuming.

When they arrived with Trixie at Georgio's office, enthusiastic hugs were exchanged. He wondered how the meeting would progress.

Chapter 6
More Decisions

When everyone was comfortably seated, Georgio asked Trixie for an update on the operations of the Recruitment Office. She reported that the entire planet had received one visit from her office and the results were very good. Now the pace had slowed and she wished to reevaluate the size of her office staff.

Georgio and Skye locked eyes and smiled. "Just what we were about to discuss," said Georgio. He shared the conversation that he and Skye had just had and asked for feedback from Trixie and the twins.

Trixie looked thoughtful and then turned to the twins. "I am reluctant to make any decisions before hearing from you. Please let me know your thoughts."

Andrea spoke first, "Leilani and I have been noticing the inevitable decline in new recruits. Once we had covered the whole planet, we believe this was bound to take place.

We recommend that one of us seek another position—and it seems that an opportunity has just presented itself."

Leilani added, "Because we are twins, we share minds often and are quite aware of each other's preferences. Therefore, there will be no hard feelings when we let you know that I am interested in transferring to Skye's command. Andrea will remain with Trixie."

Trixie confirmed that decision. "Let it be so...with Georgio's approval, of course."

Georgio retrieved a bottle of bubbly and poured celebratory drinks for everyone. "That was the easiest solving of a personnel issue that I've ever experienced. Thank you for your willingness to roll with the change," he said, toasting the Recruitment staff.

He then invited everyone to join him for lunch in the nearby pub, hoping that it would turn into a brainstorming session.

*   *   *   *   *

As they sat at a secluded table, Georgio cast a bubble to secure their privacy. Only the server would be allowed entry. After their orders had been taken, he broadened their conversation to include a wide range of topics.

Skye offered the first idea: "Greta and I are inaugurating an internship program at the Pro Bono Shop to pick up some of the slack created when I accepted my position here—but also, to increase the awareness of law school students about pro bono work.

30

Could that model be replicated in the Recruiting Office?"

Trixie thought a moment and clapped, "I think such a program would be an excellent move forward. It would definitely expand our reach and take advantage of a host of new ideas in the process. I'm excited about doing that. Thank you, Skye.

"Andrea, would you take point on designing that internship experience?" Trixie asked.

"I'd love to," Andrea smiled. "I believe Academy students will really take to the idea."

"This is a great start to our brainstorming session," praised Georgio.

"I'd like to talk about our christening sessions of Space Ships," Leilani began. "Is there some way that we could establish a routine and broadcast it so that citizens could be better informed and enjoy the experience?"

"We've been operating as if it was a crisis event, which is very non-productive," replied Georgio. "Why don't you and Preme come up with some suggestions? You are suggesting a better mode of communication—which really should be under the control of your office."

At that moment, the server returned with their orders and further brainstorming was tabled. Georgio felt very energized by this first session. He planned to ask the Communicators to schedule further sessions on a regular basis.

*   *   *   *   *

The next day, Leilani reported to Georgio's office to spend the day with Klyde, the Communicator she would be replacing. In addition to learning about her new position, she intended to run an idea past him, as well.

She was a quick study and soon felt quite comfortable with the list of duties Klyde had included on a prepared document for her. When it was time for lunch, she suggested that they walk to the nearby pub and he happily agreed.

They located an available table outside. It was a lovely day and being in the open air felt perfect. After engaging in some small talk, she began to share some of what the previous day's brainstorming session had produced.

"Since both the Pro Bono Shop and our Recruiting Office are going to be initiating internship programs—and you are moving over to the Academy President's office—I thought you might entertain the idea of establishing a formal Internship Program operating from that location. I think formalizing such a Program would attract more students to consider participating in it."

Klyde considered her proposal and promised to discuss it with Crystos once he settled into the routine of the President's Office.

32

"Would you be willing to meet with us if he shows interest in your idea?" he asked.

Leilani agreed to do so and was pleased that Klyde would carry the concept forward. As always, she mentally shared the good news with her twin, who complimented her on being proactive. Privately, Leilani felt that this change of employment would increase the range of effectiveness that she and Andrea could achieve.

Chapter 7
Coronation Eve

Shamous had been working very hard to prepare for the Coronation of Candace as the next Queen of Marinea. The ceremony—open only to invited guests— would begin in the Palace Ballroom, from which a procession would take place leading to the Throne Room. At that point, the newly-crowned Queen would ascend the Throne and receive tributes from the invited guests.

After the formalities had concluded, the Royal Family would return to the Ballroom for a private Reception, which would be followed by a Royal Procession via horses and carriages— escorted by a squadron of the Security Force— through the kingdom.

He had rejected the idea of open carriages as it might cause security concerns. Unknown to everyone, he had spelled all carriage windows to be attack-proof. While Candace would be a popular Queen, one couldn't be too careful.

Queen Candace and her mate, Consort Cyril, would lead the Royal Procession. Queen Emerita Tamara and Commander Emeritus Sean would occupy the second coach. Members of the Royal

Family were assigned to the remaining coaches.

It would be a very festive procession. Because the kingdom was under the sea, the weather could be controlled. Flowers could be seen lining the entire parade route.

Shamous had decorated the Ballroom and Throne Room in shades of blue to accent the relationship between the kingdom and the sea in which it resided. The attire of the new Queen and her court was designed to reflect that important connection.

Spinning around, he literally danced with anticipation of the day he had created. He hoped everything would go well and that Queen Candace would appreciate his efforts.

*   *   *   *   *

Candace had refused to occupy the Queen's apartment in the Palace. She did not want to displace her mother, who could still use it during her visits. She also encouraged Mia, her mother's Attendant for many years, to remain in her mother's service both in Marinea and at the Crystal Castle. Mia was pleased to comply.

It felt a little silly to ask that the Classroom be left intact, but she was hopeful that she and Cecil might have more children one day. Therefore, new quarters would need to be created and Cecil was willing to undertake that project. Cecil knew just who to ask for help: Shamous!

Cecil entered **Your Every Wish** and looked for Shamous—who emerged from his office. "How large a space do you need for your quarters?" asked Shamous. "About the same size as Queen Tamara and Commander Sean used?"

Stunned, Cecil stared at Shamous. "How did you know what I wanted?" he stammered.

"You know the name of my shop…and you are seeking my help with a wish, am I correct?" Shamous inquired.

Flushing with embarrassment, Cecil nodded. "Candace always told me that you know everything," he reported. "And now I'm a believer!"

Shamous laughed. "The Palace has a lovely open outdoor space behind the Chapel and adjacent to the Garden. What do you think of that location?"

"Outside?" mumbled Cecil. "I was thinking of somewhere inside the Palace."

"It will be," assured Shamous. "Please come back tomorrow." And he escorted Cecil to the door.

*   *   *   *   *

The next day, Cecil returned to Shamous' shop and they teleported to Palace grounds. As they neared the Garden, Cecil couldn't believe his eyes! The Palace had expanded and now covered the area he and Shamous had discussed the day before.

The first floor had a glass wall and terrace looking out at

the Garden. Entering the Palace they ascended a staircase to the second floor where a large bedroom complex and two offices also overlooked the Garden.

"This is perfect!" exclaimed Cecil. "How…"

"Does this meet your needs?" inquired Shamous.

Cecil sent a mental summons to Candace, who appeared at once. Her face showed both appreciation and wonder. "Shamous, you've done it again!" she cried, "How did you know exactly what we needed?"

"That's my job," admitted Shamous. "I'm pleased that you like it. I've moved everything from your rental into this new space. You will be able to prepare for tomorrow's Coronation right here.

"Mia will help you dress in the morning. She has agreed to stay until you hire someone to assist you—then she will return to your mother's service. I'll meet you here in the morning. Your breakfast will be served in your new quarters." And he vanished.

Candace threw her arms around Cecil and giggled. "He is always full of surprises," she assured him. Cecil picked her up and placed her on their bed. With a loving kiss, he suggested that they find the Private Dining Room and have some dinner. Feeling at home already, they wandered into the hall where a staff member was waiting to escort them to dinner.

Chapter 8
The Coronation

It was the morning of the Coronation. Candace and Cecil awakened to soft music and a soft knock at their new bedroom door. When invited, Mia entered and placed a breakfast tray on a nearby table.

Mia pointed to a hanging cord by the door, saying, "When you have finished breakfast, Your Majesty, just pull the cord and I'll return to help you dress for the Coronation." Bowing, she exited the room.

"I wonder how long it will take for me to not turn and look for my mother when I hear 'Your Majesty'?" Candace asked Cecil.

He laughed and answered, "Not long. Your mother will be a visitor to the Palace, not a resident. Your parents will be living in the Crystal Castle, as I understand it."

"I understand that," Candace commented, "but it isn't real in my mind yet. What IS real is my tummy—it's hungry!" And they moved to the table to enjoy a delicious meal.

*   *   *   *   *

After hearing the cord bell, Mia returned to assist Candace

and Cecil prepare for the Coronation. Opening the wardrobe door, she discovered that the Coronation attire had been placed there…presumably by Shamous.

She giggled because as soon as she thought Shamous' name, he was knocking at the door! Entering, Shamous waved his hand and Cecil's outfit disappeared from the wardrobe. He waved to Cecil to follow him and they left the bedroom.

"Where did they go?" Candace asked Mia.

"I think they will dress in an adjacent room, Your Majesty," Mia responded. "I will prepare a bath for you now."

After a relaxing soak, Candace stepped out of her bath and donned a soft robe. Mia tended to her hair, then assisted her into the blue Coronation gown.

"You look lovely, Your Majesty," Mia gushed.

At that moment, Shamous and Cecil returned and Cecil kissed his mate, agreeing with Mia, who reminded them that it was time to go to the Palace Ballroom and welcome the invited guests.

*   *   *   *   *

The rest of the day proceeded as Shamous had orchestrated it…with one exception. When Terra placed the Crown on Candace's head, tiny fireworks exploded all over the ceiling of the Ballroom and Candace glowed with a golden light.

Tamara moved forward to touch the pendant around Candace's

neck—and an additional ring of clear crystals appeared, encircling the rainbow ring. Candace was now officially the Queen of Marinea!

Mother and daughter embraced and tears flowed. The New Order had truly begun.

Queen Candace and Consort Cecil led a procession of family and guests into the Throne Room where she ascended the Throne. Formal gifts and tributes would be presented at this time. Afterward, everyone would return to the Ballroom for the reception.

Following the reception, the Royal Family would leave the Palace and board their carriages for the procession through the kingdom. A marching band from the Academy led the parade.

While not obvious, security was high. Members of the Security Force in plain clothes lined the streets along with Marinean citizens. There was a lot of cheering and waving. It was a very festive occasion.

Suddenly, figures in black interrupted the parade and began to attack the carriages. The spell Shamous had placed upon the carriage windows held them off and the attackers' frustration was evident.

Band members' instruments turned into weapons as they repelled the attackers. The Security Force members who were

41

part of the parade took the insurgents into custody and teleported them away.

Security Force members who were not in uniform began to practice crowd control so the parade could continue on peacefully. Very soon, order was restored.

In the second carriage, Sean was in communication with Jon, the new Commander of the Security Force. "Do we know who these insurgents are—or what they are trying to achieve?" he asked Jon.

"Not yet," replied Jon. "I'm about to interrogate those who were teleported here. Do you want to join me?"

"Definitely," Sean asserted and teleported out of the carriage.

Tamara, who was used to his disappearing act, pasted a smile on her face and waved enthusiastically to the crowd.

In the first carriage, the newly-crowned Queen Candace was shaken by the attack. Cecil tried to calm her with a spell, but his nerves wouldn't let him. Terra appeared in the coach and successfully managed to calm both of them.

"Smile at the crowd, Candace," she urged. "And wave vigorously. You need to appear calm and in control! The Security Force will deal with these bad actors!"

Candace nodded and took a deep breath. She understood what was expected of her.

Chapter 9
The Insurgents

Sean connected with Jon at the holding cells in Security Force Headquarters. Since Sean's techniques of interrogation were well-regarded, Jon indicated that he should handle these prisoners.

Once Sean had created the vid screen above the prisoners' heads, he let them know that he would be aware of whether their statements were true or false.

As he began the questioning, he noticed that he was responding to their answers more often with a cry of 'false' than with one of 'true'. It was time to cast a 'truth spell'.

The first truthful response he received was related to where these insurgents came from. He was actually not surprised to hear "Divos". There had been a suspicion in his mind that some of those spies might still be on Akura. They might not even be aware of the peace settlement that had been brokered.

Once he decided to provide the prisoners with that intel, he watched them carefully, waiting for reactions. The looks on their faces ranged from disbelief, to wary, to angry. He was saddened that not one of the prisoners believed what he had shared. There was no option presently other than to incarcerate them.

Sean advised Jon to place them in secure detention. They were a danger to the kingdom. Jon nodded in agreement and Sean teleported back to the carriage he was sharing with Tamara. Briefing her fully, he held her hand and asked if she had any other suggestions about the prisoners.

Shaking her head negatively, she made a mental note to return to that decision once they had permanently relocated to the Crystal Castle.

*   *   *   *   *

When the Royal procession had ended and returned to the Palace, the Royal Family went to the Private Dining Room for lunch.

Shamous had added that gathering to the day's schedule once the attack had been repelled. He knew that it would be necessary for everyone's well-being to talk about the incident.

Candace looked pale. Tamara was worried that she was viewing the attack as being directed to her personally. Once everyone was seated comfortably and given their orders to the servers, Tamara stood to get their attention.

"One of my roles as Queen Emerita will be to share my experience. I'm doing it now," she proclaimed. "From what Sean has learned from his interrogation of the prisoners, this attack was a political act by the spies from Divos who had not as yet been apprehended.

"They were unaware of the peace treaty that had been ratified by all parties and, it seems, are unwilling to believe that it has taken place. Consequently, they will be held in custody until we can figure out how to help them understand."

Looking at her daughter, she continued, "I want to emphasize that Candace, as the new Queen of Marinea, was in no way a deliberate target of their anger. The procession was, in my opinion, a convenient opportunity to express it to all of us through a single action."

Tamara put her hand on Candace's shoulder and added, "Candace will be an excellent Queen. She has served repeatedly in her role as Queen-Designate with distinction. I give her my blessing and ask for your loyalty in this new transition."

There was a standing ovation as the two Queens, past and present, shared a hug. Tamara was pleased to see that Candace had regained her poise and confidence.

*   *   *   *   *

That evening, Tamara and Sean entered the Garden for one of their relaxing walks. "The Crystal Castle has a small garden,"

Tamara remarked. "I would like to expand it and include a boat ride like we have here."

Sean nodded. "I think that's an excellent idea, Dear. I would miss it otherwise. When do you want to return to the Crystal Castle?"

"I just want to make sure that Candace is settled in her new role," answered Tamara. "I'll let you know." They continued strolling through the Garden until they reached the boat dock. "Let's take a short ride now. It's a beautiful night."

Boarding the boat, they looked up to see a white tornado approaching. "I think that decision may not be ours to make," Sean told her, putting his arms around her shoulders.

The tornado scooped them up and disappeared into the sky. Shamous was watching from the Garden, thinking to himself, *"I'd better keep an eye on Candace. The New Order has definitely begun."*

*   *   *   *   *

Tamara and Sean soon found themselves standing before the Crystal Castle. Rogere and Elsa emerged and welcomed them 'home'.

"Why are we here?" asked Tamara with a catch in her throat. "I wanted to remain near Candace until she was calm and in control."

"That is why we sent for you," soothed Elsa. "As long as you were with her, she would rely on you and slow her own development. It's difficult to let a child go, but it's in her best interest."

Sean's arm around Tamara's shoulder tightened as tears formed in her eyes. She knew the truth of what Elsa said—but she didn't have to like it!

"We were monitoring you and heard your plans for a larger garden with a boat," said Rogere. "Shall we begin that project?"

Tamara wiped her eyes and nodded. That would be just the distraction she needed.

Chapter 10
Candace 2.0

When Shamous knocked at the door of the Royal Office, Candace bid him enter. As he did so, he subtly cast a calming spell before he began to tell her that her parents had been summoned.

"Summoned!" she cried, defeating his spell. "But why? I need Mama here for advice—and hugs!"

"*Exactly why she was taken,*" he guessed mentally. Aloud, he responded, "No, you don't. You deftly held the reins of the kingdom when you were Queen-Designate. It's now time for you to accept your full authority. You know you can call me if you have a question, but I really don't expect to hear from you. You are a capable young woman, Candace."

Shamous bowed and vanished.

*   *   *   *   *

Candace sat and began to sort through the papers on her desk. She noticed a new photo of herself and her parents sitting there and thought, "Thank you, Shamous."

A knock at her door disturbed her concentration. "Enter," she called.

Jon walked in and took a seat. "I've come to report the status of our new inmates in person. After Sean questioned them, they were very resistant and refused to believe that a peace treaty had been ratified. Sean advised me to keep them in custody until their attitude changes. Do you agree, Your Majesty?"

"At this time, I do," Candace told him. "We will be assessing this situation often. Please keep me advised if anything changes...and please call me Candace. You and I don't need formality. We've known each other all my life. You will be one of my closest advisers."

Jon turned to leave, then sat down again. "Do you have any questions for me, Candace?" he asked. "We have both been thrown into a new situation, even though we have experience to build upon. Let's help each other get through this seismic shift that we are trying to navigate. Remember that your mother had Sean as her mate—and he was Security Force Commander when they wed. Your mate has the ability to rule a kingdom, but that is a different set of skills than being a Commander. So please consider me at your service whenever you need my military skills and experience."

Candace smiled and thanked Jon for his generosity. She rose and gave him a hug before he teleported away.

*   *   *   *   *

Candace asked Mia to arrange that dinner would be served in their quarters. She was looking forward to the intimacy of dining with her mate in a private setting.

Cecil had returned to Freedom for the day in order to bring his twin up-to-date on the conditions in that kingdom. Fortunately, there were no crises at the moment and he could help Cyrus acclimate to his new position as Ruler.

By the end of the day, the Rulership had smoothly passed to Cyrus and Cyril was both pleased and relieved. The kingdom of Freedom would be in capable hands.

By the time he teleported back to the Palace in Marinea, he had successfully divested his mind of the kingdom of Freedom and was ready to assume the post of Consort to the Queen.

Checking with a staff member, he was informed that the Queen had ordered a private dinner to be served in their bed chamber. Smiling, he hurried to meet her there and was rewarded with a loving kiss.

*   *   *   *   *

Dinner had just arrived, so Candace and Cecil gave it priority. After Cecil poured some bubbly, they toasted the beginning of a new adventure for both of them. Cecil relaxed when he saw that Candace was looking toward the future. Her prior anxiety had melted away…he didn't know why, but he was glad of it.

Candace had participated in a type of internship when she was Queen-Designate. He had no such benefit as he approached his new role. There were uncharted waters ahead, but the love they shared would see them through. He was sure of that.

Neither of them sensed that they were being observed by a cloaked Shamous in the corner. Shamous had cast a love spell in the room to make this evening special.

He intended to keep a close eye on them for a while—lending a helping hand when needed. He rather enjoyed the opportunity to be a 'Fairy Godfather'!

The evening progressed just as he had hoped. When Candace and Cecil had finished dinner, Shamous tactfully teleported out, ensuring their privacy before he left.

Tomorrow would be soon enough to face the realities of the New Order. Tonight was for love.

Chapter 11
Changing Roles

The next day, Candace and Cyril had breakfast in their quarters and then he escorted her to her office. The pile of papers she had been reading yesterday was still waiting for her—and a new pile had mysteriously appeared next to it! She looked at her desk with dismay!

"When I took over as Queen-Designate," she moaned, "there wasn't this amount of paperwork. What has happened?"

"I'm guessing that your mother was absorbed in creating the ideal Coronation Day for you...and let it pile up," Cecil suggested. "Let's talk about it for a minute.

"Your mother had a Consort who was also full-time as Security Force Commander. That relationship was very useful in many ways. But you and I have different strengths," Cecil pointed out. "We can design your reign differently."

"How do you mean?" asked Candace.

"When you need Security advice," he continued, "You have Jon available as a Consultant. When you need another hand sorting through paperwork and other Royal duties, you could hire an assistant—or I could be that assistant. It's entirely up to you, of course."

"That's brilliant, Darling!" Candace cried out! "The position of Consort has no job description, so we can make it whatever works best for us! I love it…Which pile do you want?"

Laughing, they divided the piles between them…and Candace ordered a second desk to be brought to her office. She felt like the challenge she was facing had been cut in helf—which it actually was!

*   *   *   *   *

She was surprised how quickly the piles of paper diminished in size. As Queen-Designate, she had found the work lonely and sometimes overwhelming. But now, they could bounce ideas off each other, tell jokes, and even steal a kiss or two!

They worked so well as a team that by the time they left for lunch, all the paperwork had been handled. The new desk had arrived quickly…she suspected Shamous had a role in that. Even more suspicious was the office itself. She was certain that the dimensions had changed; it seemed so much larger!

Cecil solved that puzzle for her. He remembered that there had been two offices—one for each of them—adjacent to their quarters. They were located directly above the Royal Office of the Queen. Somehow the total square footage of the Royal Office had been enlarged to match those offices. He agreed that Shamous probably had something to do with it.

Since they had worked so efficiently through the morning, they felt no guilt at taking the afternoon off. Cecil suggested that they leave the Palace and eat lunch at their favorite pub. Candace seconded that idea and they walked into town, hand-in-hand.

It was such a lovely day that they decided to grab an outside table. Beyond the dome covering the kingdom, the ocean was drifting calmly by. Colorful fish could be seen swimming overhead.

Candace thought to herself that it was wonderful to be able to have special time with Cecil. She had missed the closeness when he was so far away governing the kingdom of Freedom.

A small pang of guilt popped into her mind and she rapidly dismissed it. She missed her mother's nearness…but she was totally enjoying having her mate close by. There were definite advantages to being Queen, she decided.

Sighing, Candace covered Cecil's hand with her own. Their server arrived with their lunch and a special bottle of bubbly that Cecil had ordered. Toasting a successful first day of her official reign, they gazed into each other's eyes and personally had similar thoughts about how to spend the afternoon.

*   *   *   *   *

The next day, they expected a repeat of the first day…but that was not to be. A knock at the Royal Office door turned out to announce their daughter, Joy—who had a request.

"Mama," began Joy, "now that I am the Queen-Designate…and Savvy will follow me in that role…we thought it would be wise to arrange some time to shadow you. Not immediately, of course. I know you need to be comfortable in your new role, but I wanted to bring the idea to your attention."

Candace hugged her daughter and led her over to the couch. "I think that's a very reasonable request, Joy. When I became Queen-Designate, I felt like I had been tossed into a pool and I didn't know how to swim! I'll let you know when I feel ready to grant your request." Joy returned her mother's hug and promised to relay the message to Savvy.

Rising, she met her father half-way and shared another hug. As she prepared to exit, she looked over her shoulder and suggested that they have a family dinner sometime soon. And then she was gone.

Chapter 12
At the Castle

Tamara and Sean were seated at a table in their quarters, watching a flat vid screen. This device was new to both of them…it could display images from anywhere in the universe. They would be able to keep track of what was happening regardless of distance or Time.

What they had just finished watching was the meeting between Candace and Joy about shadowing. "Joy has always been several steps ahead of me," commented Tamara. "Her idea has a lot of merit. I, too, felt overwhelmed when I became Queen due to my father's retirement."

"But you handled it well," praised Sean.

"I was under a lot of unnecessary stress that could have been avoided. Obviously, Candace felt that stress, too. I hope she doesn't wait too long to grant Joy's request," she remarked.

"I agree," said Sean. "One never knows when the wheel of Fate will turn."

A knock at the door announced the arrival of Rogere and Elsa. "We just wanted to let you know that a new wing of the

Castle has been completed for the retired Super Beings. They are being relocated now," informed Rogere.

"I didn't know that was happening," Sean complained. "I assumed they would be living here near to us so we could consult them if needed."

"We thought it would be advisable to have distance between you," Elsa explained. "Have you forgotten how self-absorbed they are? Do you remember the chaos of the game?"

"I certainly remember being put in the dungeon," laughed Tamara. "I think you made a wise decision. Do they realize why they are being moved?"

"I sincerely doubt it," answered Rogere. "They are too busy decorating their new digs. You haven't been on their minds at all—no surprise."

"If you want to ask them anything, you can use your new device to contact—or spy—on them," Elsa pointed out.

Tamara nodded, "I'm comfortable with that. My memory is quite clear about our past interactions. While they seemed welcoming when we arrived here, I never really trusted them."

"Nor did I," agreed Sean. "By the way, is there any way to use this device to see into the future? I feel a bit handicapped not being able to do so since Savvy and Starr seem to access it quite easily."

"That's a good question," commented Rogere. "You are still thinking strategically."

"We anticipate that your military training and background will come in handy…and soon," added Elsa. "But to answer your question, your device is linked to your brain waves. All you have to do is think a question and it will respond."

"Amazing!" Tamara exclaimed. She was still for a moment, then the screen of the device showed Candace and Cecil holding a pair of twins. "I knew it!" Tamara cried. "I had a feeling that more children were in their future."

Sean sighed, "Given the skills and Generations of their first two grandchildren, I wonder what the next babes will be like."

Elsa giggled, "Time will tell!"

Rogere groaned and led her from the room.

*   *   *   *   *

It was difficult for Tamara and Sean to tear themselves away from their new 'toy'. They spent the rest of the day peeking into the lives of their family members. It was gratifying to find that there were no crises anywhere. Tamara was worried about Elsa's comment that Sean's military experience would come in handy SOON.

When she shared that concern with him, he advised her not

to worry unnecessarily. "If there is something coming that we have to deal with, we will do so. It doesn't help to imagine what it might be."

Privately, Tamara realized that his attitude was part of the military expertise that would successfully handle whatever challenge the future might present.

Leaning her head on his shoulder, she felt herself relax. She wondered—as she had so often in her life—what lucky star she was born under that brought this wonderful man into her life.

Sean kissed her and asked, "Shall we go into our Garden and check on the progress of the renovation?"

Taking his arm, they teleported into the Garden. Tamara gasped at the beauty displayed before them. There appeared to be flowers everywhere—from the ground cover up to the top of the tallest trees.

As they strolled down the path, they saw light being reflected from some water ahead of them. It was a river, just like the one they had enjoyed in Marinea. And there was a boat tied up to a dock.

This boat was more deluxe than the one they had left behind. It looked like they would be able to sleep aboard it, soothed by the lapping of water all around.

A canopy of stars twinkled overhead. Tamara didn't know if they were real or simulated, but she really didn't care. It was so beautiful!

She grabbed Sean's hand and ran to the dock. Leaping aboard the boat, they settled in two comfortable reclining chairs. Still holding hands, they felt the motion of the water and two glasses of bubbly appeared in cup holders on the arms of their chairs.

What a wonderful way to end the day!

Chapter 13
The Queen's Office

Candace and Cecil were hard at work doing the kingdom's business. But it wasn't really work for them. They enjoyed each other's company so much that it brought them joy to share the process of governing.

An urgent knock at the door disturbed their reverie. Without being invited, Jon burst into the room. "We have an emergency situation," he cried. "Another group of spies that we had not identified have attacked the Security Force holding cells and freed the prisoners!"

Candace gasped and Cecil rose, asking "Was anybody hurt?"

Jon responded, "Nothing life-threatening, but there were some injuries. Do you have a way to contact Sean?"

"I do," admitted Candace. "I'll send Da a mental message right now." She sat still and concentrated. In a few minutes, both Tamara and Sean were present in the office.

"This must be the event that needs your experience, Dear," Tamara pronounced. "It has happened sooner than we expected."

Jon hurriedly repeated what he had already told Candace and Cecil. Sean advised him to summon Kert to join them. Perhaps he would have an idea of where the spies might be hiding since they were all from the same planet.

Kert arrived in a few minutes and was quickly briefed by Jon. He had never given any thought to whether spies from Divos might still be active on Akura. The shock on his face bore testimony to that.

However, he did remember that both major kingdoms shared a few attributes: the residents enjoyed living near water…and often took up residence in caves. Sean found that intel very valuable and offered to send his local birds on a reconnaissance flight. Both water and caves were in good supply on Akura.

Sean and Jon directed the birds to cruise the air around Alteria. In the time that had elapsed since the prisoners were freed, they would have been able to hop on a Bubble Train and reach Alteria. From there, they could have access to the rest of the planet. It was imperative that they be found before that would be possible.

The eyes of everyone in the Royal Office were glued to the several vid screens. Sean decided to try a different approach and murmured a spell softly. One vid screen began to rewind to show the attack on the holding cells. He paid close attention to what was displayed, shouting "I was right!" when the Bubble Train arrived at the station; Both the spies and the liberated prisoners climbed aboard.

With this confirmation in mind, Sean asked the birds to focus on the Bubble Train station in Alteria. As he watched, the train pulled into the station and the culprits exited. At this point, the replay had caught up to real time and the whereabouts of the fugitives was known.

Jon sent an urgent message to the Space Force Base on Alteria and mobilized Security Force members to apprehend the culprits. Within minutes, that had been accomplished and the fugitives were back in custody, having been teleported back to Security Force holding cells.

"Elsa was correct, Dear," Tamara smiled and commented to Sean, "Your military skills did need to be accessed." Turning to the Royal couple, she added, "We are always available to you when needed. Don't hesitate to call on us." Giving Candace hugs, Tamara and Sean disappeared. Kert was the next to leave.

Jon bowed to Candace and Cecil, thanking them for their assistance and teleported away.

"Well," remarked Candace, "that certainly brought an exciting start to our day. Shall we finish our paperwork and go out for lunch?"

With a devilish look in his eyes, Cecil agreed, mentioning that he had plans for the afternoon. Blushing, Candace returned to her chair and winked at him.

*   *   *   *   *

When Candace and Cecil arrived at the pub for lunch, they found Joy and her two children already seated at an outside table. Two empty chairs beckoned to them.

"Were you expecting us?" asked Cecil.

"Yes, Da," answered Joy. "We need to talk."

"Will Kert be joining us?" asked Candace.

"No, Mama," Joy replied. "After being with you this morning, he had to return to Base."

"What do we need to talk about?" asked Cecil.

"Let's order first, Da," suggested Joy. "We can wait until we've eaten lunch."

Once their orders had arrived and enjoyed, Cecil offered to send for a bottle of bubbly. Joy held up her hand and cautioned, "I don't think so, Da. Let's talk first."

Cecil turned to Candace, a puzzled look on his face. Mentally he asked her, "*Everyone loves bubbly. What is going on?*"

"*I suspect we will find out soon,*" replied Candace. "*Let's see what they have to say.*"

"Grandma," Savvy began, "Do you remember the story about when Mama and I were on the training mission and I informed her that there was an unlawful presence on board?"

"Of course, Dear," smiled Candace, "and it turned out to be Starr!"

Starr could contain himself no longer. "It's happening again, Grandma. I've seen it! And this time, it's not Mama."

Crystal Saga Series 4

4 – Adapting to Change

D. E. Weingand

Prologue

My name is Terra. I am the Head Watcher and liaison to the planet Akura during the establishment of the New Order. I work closely with the Creator Being.

I am wed to Trident, the Marinean Ambassador to the kingdom of Alteria, and former Prince—then King—of Marinea. I am also the mother of Tamara (now Queen Emerita) and Trina (who works in the Academy).

This is a very difficult time for the residents of our planet, Akura. The cosmology that everyone grew up learning featured Super Beings who lived in the Crystal Castle and had progeny through the ages. However, they were very self-absorbed and also caused various conflicts.

The Creator Being, having recognized how the universe was changing, decided to retire them and now they live in a separate wing of the Crystal Castle. My daughter, Tamara, and her mate, Commander Sean of the Marinean Security Force, have been promoted to serve as the new Super Beings. They have received Emerita/Emeritus status and now reside in the Crystal Castle.

This huge change has precipitated a deluge of additional changes throughout the planet. This is why the Creator Being appointed me as Liaison so that I could monitor the changes and help with the actions necessary to move forward.

My Granddaughter, Candace, formerly the Queen-Designate, has now been crowned Queen as her mother has moved into the Crystal Castle. She and her mate, Cecil (the former Ruler of the kingdom of Freedom) have already learned to work together in governing Marinea. Cecil's experience as a Ruler is proving to be very important.

Changes are now underway in the staffing of the Space Force, the Security Force and the Academy. I am trying to be as helpful as possible in assisting my extended family cope with their responses to these fundamental shifts in our lives.

So far, I am pleased with the leadership being shown and I am grateful for it. While change is never easy, change of this magnitude is tremendously challenging. I have faith in my family members and look forward to assisting them navigate what is happening all around them.

I am not alone in this endeavor. I have detected Shamous' hand at work already. He is a loyal friend and extremely talented…as well as fun to watch!

Chapter 1
Shamous

The good will that Shamous feels for the Royal Family of Marinea has no bounds. He has contributed significantly by adding his magic to special occasions—most often for weddings, but also for Coronations…and remodeling of both residences and public spaces. His talents are so remarkable that the Royal Family is most appreciative.

This time, however, he has decided to be involved in a long-term project: monitoring Queen Candace and Consort Cecil as they struggle to negotiate the challenges presented by the changes that are happening everywhere they look.

The Royal Couple was never aware that they were being observed by Shamous. He kept himself cloaked whenever he was in their presence. Their seamless flow into handling the piles of paperwork pleased him. They worked well together, with love smoothing the way.

If he didn't have to intervene at all, that would be fine with him. He enjoyed watching the ebb and flow of ideas between them. It was obvious that they enhanced their personal creativity by sharing and solving problems. To his knowledge, this style of governing was unique on Akura. Other kingdoms, including his own, could learn from it.

As lunchtime approached, Cecil extended his hand to Candace and drew her into his arms. A deep kiss rewarded them and they decided to take a stroll in the Garden before ordering lunch.

Finding a vacant bench, they settled into it. A wave of Candace's hand and a server came toward them. She requested that lunch be served on the boat; the server bowed and returned to the Palace. Rising, they continued their walk, arriving shortly at the boat dock.

Surprised, they discovered a table already set with bubbly and two glasses. After sitting and toasting each other, the couple took in the lovely view and relaxed. When lunch was served, Candace thanked the server for the wonderful service. She didn't understand the confused look on his face; She didn't know that Shamous had produced the setting. It was his first intervention.

*   *   *   *   *

After lunch, they were meandering back to the Palace when a light rain began to fall. It was a pre-planned watering of the Garden. Shamous waved his hand and a bubble kept them dry as they laughed and ran for shelter.

Entering the Palace, they became aware that their clothes were dry. At that point, they began to suspect that Shamous was in the vicinity. Smiling, Shamous chose to let them wonder and teleported away.

*   *   *   *   *

Shamous arrived at Kronos in a flash of light. He found his twin brother in the dining hall, finishing his lunch. They embraced and Shamous sat down to order lunch for himself.

After enjoying his lunch, Shamous began to tell his twin, King Rupert II, of what he had observed while monitoring Queen Candace. Rupert was intrigued with the concept of shared governance—just as Shamous had expected.

"What do you think about trying it out here in Kronos?" asked Shamous. "I could visit more often and we could tackle those piles of boring paperwork together."

"It would be grand to see you more often, Brother," Rupert admitted. "And I certainly could use some help with that paperwork, as well as other aspects of governing. How soon do you want to start?"

"I still want to monitor Queen Candace—and I have my shop to manage," Shamous reminded him. "I need a few weeks to make arrangements. What if I return in a moon's time?"

"That sounds fine," agreed Rupert. "It will be so nice to have you here for longer periods of time. And it will be good

3

training for you so that when you take over, you have experience in how things work around here."

Exchanging hugs, the twins bid each other farewell…with the promise of reconnecting soon. Shamous teleported back to his shop to alert his Assistant about the change that was about to take place.

*   *   *   *   *

Candace and Cecil returned to their desks. There were still piles of paperwork—although smaller—needing their attention. They worked diligently for a few hours, stretched, and sent for some snacks to sustain them until dinner.

A soft knock at the door announced the arrival of Joy and Savvy. "Mama," Joy began, "Starr has encouraged us to visit and ask whether you are ready to let us shadow you. He told us that you and Da have a new system to lighten the boring workload of governing. We'd like to know more."

Savvy added, "Starr has also informed us that Shamous has been shadowing you already. If he can learn from you, we would like to learn also."

"Where is Starr?" inquired Cecil.

"He's waiting in the hall for us," admitted Joy. "Shall I get him?"

"Please do," Cecil replied. "I want to ask him some questions."

When Starr came in, he looked at his father with some trepidation. "What questions, Da?" he asked.

"How do you know Shamous has been shadowing us?" Cecil pressed.

"I stopped by one day," Starr explained. "I cloaked myself so as not to disturb you. Then I saw Shamous, also cloaked, standing against the wall watching you."

"You could see through his cloaking spell?" Cecil continued.

"Of course," Starr answered. "It's one of my Generation skills. Savvy can do it, too."

Cecil sighed, "It's important that the Queen is able to rule with privacy. How can we make that happen?"

"I can put a secure privacy bubble around this room, Da," Starr responded. "Do you want me to do that?"

"Immediately!" hollered Cecil.

Chapter 2
The Issue of Privacy

Starr chanted softly, waved his hands, and a dense fog poured through the Royal Office. When it dissipated, Starr asked Savvy to cloak herself. She tried but was not able to do so.

Starr smiled and said, "All is secure, Da."

"Now I want you to report to Commander Jon in Security Force Headquarters," Cecil ordered. "Explain what has just transpired and discuss with him how the Queen's privacy has been breached."

Starr looked ill, but complied by teleporting out.

Candace looked worried and sent a mental summons to Shamous, who appeared almost immediately.

"How can I be of service, Your Majesty?" he inquired.

She looked at him sorrowfully, "Shamous, we have been informed that you have been spying on us while cloaked. What do you have to say about that?"

Flushing, Shamous apologized and tried to explain his motivation. "I understand your purpose, but do you not agree that this Office must be off limits to anyone not invited, regardless of their good intentions?" Candace asked.

"I assure you, my objective was your safety, Your Majesty," he insisted. "We have so much sudden change to deal with." And then he related how impressed he was with the new governing strategy Candace and Cecil had invented. "In fact, my brother and I are going to try to implement it in Kronos starting next month."

Candace leaned back in her chair; it was so hard to be upset with Shamous. "Do me a favor, Shamous," she asked. "Please cloak yourself right now."

He tried…then tried again, but was not successful. "I don't know what's wrong," he complained. "I've never had trouble doing it before."

Smiling, she advised, "My grandson made this office secure. You might want to talk to him about doing it for the Royal Office in Kronos when you start the new governing model there. Privacy is essential to Royal decision-making."

Shamous bowed, extended his apologies once more…and vanished.

*   *   *   *   *

When Starr returned to the Royal Office, he reported that Jon was intrigued with his ability to make locations secure. "He told me that cloaking has always been a problem for the Security Force. He appointed me as a new Consultant for the Force, which I was glad to accept."

Cecil shook his head. His attempt at discipline had morphed into a golden opportunity for his grandson. Joy and Savvy were clapping with delight at how everything turned out. They were happy for Starr.

Now it was the girls' turn to apply some pressure. Looking plaintively at Candace, they asked once again if they could shadow her. Leaning back in her chair, she capitulated.

"I suppose you can," Candace agreed. "But there have to be some ground rules."

"What are those?" Savvy wondered.

"Rules that must be in place every time you are shadowing—such as, silence and distance. I can't have you talking or hovering because it will distract me from what I am doing," Candace explained.

"If you have questions, you can take notes and we will establish a time to go over them," she continued. "In other words, I can't be aware of your presence—or I won't be able to do my job properly.

"Are these conditions acceptable?" Candace asked.

"Yes," the girls answered together. "But it would have been easier if we could have cloaked."

"Perhaps," Candace admitted, "but I also need to know your whereabouts. You can begin shadowing tomorrow, but you must also leave the room if I tell you to. Some things taking place in this Office must be completely private."

"Can I shadow you, too?" asked Starr.

"No, dear," Candace answered. "Queen Tamara established a Matriarchy. Unless and until that changes, the succession will pass through the female line.

"You can learn from your mother and sister by having private conversations with them outside this Office," she continued. "Security protocols must always be in place."

Starr nodded, sadness in his eyes. He acknowledged to himself that this was why, when he visited the future, there were only queens ruling Marinea, not kings. He hadn't realized until now that he harbored a secret ambition to be a king. Perhaps the Security Force would be a better venue for his latent ambitions.

Right now, he decided to visit Trident, his distant relative, who was once the King of Marinea. He wanted to find out why that was no longer possible. Exiting the Royal Office, he teleported to Alteria. While he was there, he would also check out opportunities in the Space Force.

Chapter 3
Starr's Research

Trident was working in his Ambassador's office when he heard a knock at the door. Calling "Enter", he was surprised to see Starr opening the door.

Standing, he gestured to a nearby chair. "What a surprise, son," Trident welcomed. "I'm delighted to see you."

Starr made himself comfortable and subtly cast a calming spell so that Trident would not be upset by the questions he was about to ask. Trident was aware of Starr's agenda, but he played along. Terra had alerted him just a short time ago. Being wed to the Head Watcher had proved helpful many times.

As a young person without diplomatic skills, Starr plunged ahead with his questions and concerns. Before answering, Trident decided to help the boy understand his personal history as a Prince and then King…and why he chose to leave that behind in order to become an Ambassador.

He emphasized how the duties of being a Royal had kept him away from his own family, which he regretted. Sharing the saga of the fake king of Marinea and the twin brother he never knew as a child, Trident's eyes teared up.

His life goal had always been to be a proper steward of Marinea and, ultimately, he found a better purpose for that desire and goal as an Ambassador.

Starr sat, transfixed. He had no prior knowledge of Trident's pre-Ambassador life. Although he was aware Trident had been a King, all the rest of this intel was new to him. Feeling confused, and more than a little embarrassed, he apologized for the intrusion and stood, intending to leave. But Trident would have none of it.

At that moment, Terra appeared in the office, sitting in a chair next to Starr. "Starr, open your mind to me. I have intel to share with you," she implored.

Starr complied and his face registered shock and sadness. "I never realized how your family was impacted by your sense of duty," he admitted. "I guess being a King is not just pomp and circumstance."

"Yes, Starr," Trident agreed. "It's very complicated. When Tamara became Queen, I worried about how she would handle it— but she was born to be a Queen, and was so much more effective in that role than I could ever have been. My talents seem better suited to diplomacy."

Starr thanked Trident and Terra for treating him as an adult and being forthright in their answering of his questions. "I appreciate both of you and your efforts to help me understand. Please come and visit Marinea soon. There are more changes ahead." And he vanished.

Trident hugged Terra, looking at her with questions in his eyes. "More changes?" he asked. "What am I missing?"

*   *   *   *   *

Starr returned to Marinea with a feeling of peace and satisfaction with his life. After his meeting with Trident and Terra, he realized that his ambition to be a King had vanished. That would definitely not be the path he should take. Hopefully, his appointment as a Consultant in the Security Force would suggest a more appropriate path for his future.

Meanwhile, he needed to pursue his latest discovery: He was about to have a cousin and no one other than Savvy knew it. He wondered where Savvy might be now; they needed to talk.

He extended his senses outward, looking for a trace of her. In a few minutes, he found her…she was still in the Royal Office with Queen Candace. He hoped she had not divulged his secret knowledge. Sending her a mental plea, he asked her to meet him at the pub.

When he arrived at the pub, he saw that Mama was with her at an outside table. Grabbing a chair, he sat at the table with them.

"Why the urgent message, Starr?" asked Savvy. "What's going on?"

"I went to Alteria to talk to Trident," he began. "And his mate, Terra, was there, too."

"I don't understand," commented Savvy. "It's nice that you saw them, but why the urgency?"

"Did you tell the Queen anything about my secret knowledge?" Starr asked directly.

"No," Savvy said. "I figured that was your news to tell. Mama and I were shadowing the Queen and we were not allowed to talk. That's one of her rules."

Joy interrupted, "What are you two saying? Is there something you know that I don't?"

"I almost spilled it at our lunch with Grandma and Grandpa," admitted Starr. "But the time didn't seem right and I let it go."

"Starr," insisted Joy, "you are being vague. What secret are you hiding?"

"Mama," confessed Starr, "the Queen is with child."

"You did tell us, Dear," Joy reminded him. "Did you forget? You told us at that lunch."

14

"I know," he admitted, "but then I quickly erased the memory. I restored yours just now. The Queen—Grandma—still isn't aware. We really should let her know…and she definitely should be advised not to drink bubbly."

"You can erase and restore memories just like that?" sighed Joy. "What a powerful skill you have, Starr. How do you suggest we let Mama in on this secret?"

"I don't know," Starr replied softly. "I wasn't sure how to handle it. I hoped you would have an idea."

Chapter 4
The Secret

Joy and her children decided to order lunch before returning to the Palace. During their meal, Starr confessed that he went to Alteria because he was upset that he was not in the Order of Succession—and couldn't ever be King.

"But after listening to Trident and Terra, I realized that I am not suited to that life path," he admitted. "I intend to pursue opportunities with the Security Force, and possibly the Space Force at some point." Shoveling a huge bite of food into his mouth, he waited for some reaction from his mother and sister.

"I'm not surprised, my Son," commented Joy. "Nor am I," added Savvy. "Your talents are so extensive—you would be bored silly dealing with the minutiae of governing."

"So I've been spinning my wheels feeling abused for nothing? Terrific!" he pouted.

"Son," pressed Joy, "You have accelerated your physical growth but your emotional growth has yet to catch up. You must be patient and kind with yourself; Let all parts of you reach a balanced state."

"I struggled with achieving that balance myself, Starr," Savvy admitted. "It's not easy, but it definitely is important. Now, how shall we approach Candace and Cecil with your secret.?"

*   *   *   *   *

They shared ideas for hours without arriving at a decision. "What if…we invite them to a surprise baby shower?" offered Savvy.

"Won't they want to know who is having that baby?" objected Starr.

"That's part of the surprise!" Joy decided. "I like it!"

"Then let's do it!" approved Savvy. "Who else should we invite?"

"Let's limit it to the Order of Succession," advised Starr. "If we invite Cyrus, the secret will be figured out."

"We can invite the whole family…to arrive an hour later!" suggested Joy.

"That's sneaky, Mama!" cried Savvy, "and brilliant!"

"I have another idea," offered Starr. "What if we invite Candace and Cecil to a dinner with fortune cookies? We can put the same fortune in all the cookies so there's no mistake."

Joy nodded, "Actually, I like that better. I'll phone Mama tomorrow and set a date for the dinner. Once we confirm the date and time, you two can send invites to the rest of the family. On your invitations, you can call it a family gathering."

"That's settled, then," said Savvy, raising her glass. "To party planning!"

Around the corner, Shamous was listening. He was cloaked, but he was not forbidden to do so in public situations. He would be an additional partygoer, he decided.

*   *   *   *   *

Joy contacted her parents and invited them to dinner. She stressed that she had missed them since they assumed Royal duties. Playing the guilt card was not part of her repertoire, but she wasn't above playing it either. She could tell from their response that it was working.

As soon as she had firm commitments about date, time and place, she sent a mental message to her children, authorizing them to invite the rest of the family—one hour later!

The plans were proceeding nicely. They would gather in the Palace's Private Dining Room for the convenience of her parents in two days' time. Since Starr had some skills that she did not, she asked him to decorate the venue. She took responsibility for the menu and placed orders for all the favorite foods that her parents enjoyed. On many levels, Joy was really looking forward to this occasion.

To be fair, she intended to let Starr take charge of the evening's agenda. It was his secret, after all, that would be disclosed.

*   *   *   *   *

Two days later, when Joy entered the Private Dining Room, she was delightfully surprised by the decor. Starr was waiting for her, but he confessed that he actually hadn't needed to do any decorating. He thought the room was great just as it was. Joy laughed and called out, "Shamous, reveal yourself!"

She saw a shimmer in the corner and Shamous came into focus. He looked at her sheepishly, saying "I'm glad you like it."

Walking over to him, she gave him a hug—but admonished him to leave now and return when the rest of the family converged in a little over an hour. "No cloaking in the Queen's presence," she reminded him.

Nodding in agreement, Shamous vanished. He already knew what to do. However, he had escaped just in time. Candace and Cecil were entering the Private Dining Room. Savvy followed them. She had been waiting at the door.

Now that her children and parents were present, Joy directed them to an extravagantly decorated table. Candace and Cecil looked quite surprised; the Private Dining Room did not usually 'do' fancy.

A bottle of sparkling cider stood in an ice bucket next to the table. Starr poured glasses for everyone, suggesting that this would be a festive occasion, especially for them. The rest of the room was empty.

Starr smiled and released their memories of that long-ago pub lunch. Candace blushed, but Cecil looked confused—he had not been at that pub occasion. Waving his hand, Starr revealed his secret, written in fireworks across the room. Cecil kissed Candace deeply, then asked, "Is this true?" She nodded, replying, "Apparently so. Starr is truthful."

Glasses were raised in a toast. Everyone now knew why sparkling cider was present, rather than bubbly. The festivities had begun… the doors opened to admit the rest of the family—and Shamous!

Chapter 5
More Changes

Tamara and Sean had been pleased to be invited to the celebration. They marveled at Starr's ability to detect another babe about to enter the world, especially when it was so early in its genesis. Of course, everyone wanted to know the babe's gender. Starr was very discreet and asked the Queen whether she wanted that intel shared at this time. She allowed him to disclose it.

It was another girl! Starr personally wished the babe was a boy, but another girl was certainly appropriate in a matriarchy. However, he was not comfortable with sharing his secret. Something wasn't quite right. He extended his senses once more and found out why: Grandma was having twins! One babe must have been lying in front of the other in his first reading.

Clinking a glass, he immediately corrected his intel and the family stood, clapping. Tamara smiled. Her tablet in the Crystal Castle had shown her two babes. When Starr shared the corrected intel and specified twins, he also announced that the twins were fraternal: one girl and one boy! When he said 'boy', his grin was so wide; he was obviously pleased.

There had been many sets of twins born in the family. Tamara caught Starr looking at her intently. He came over and sat beside her, whispering in her ear that she, too, was carrying twins. Tamara was fascinated that once again, the number FOUR was active. However, she mentally asked Starr to let Candace have the spotlight this day and keep his latest secret to himself until she authorized it. Starr nodded his compliance.

"Thank you for letting me know, Starr," Tamara added. "That's an important talent that you have! Can you detect any other babes-to-be in the room?"

Starr closed his eyes and sent his senses throughout the room, Then he shook his head negatively. "One more thing, Starr," Tamara continued. "Can you tell if mine are boys or girls?" Starr nodded and, with a big smile, responded, "Just like the others...one of each!"

*　　*　　*　　*　　*

After dinner ended, Tamara and Sean decided to take a walk in the Garden. Tamara was pleased with her decision to create a garden similar to this one—but she had to admit that the one in the Crystal Castle was more beautiful!

Instead of looking for a vacant bench, they walked to the boat dock and sat there, looking at the water. But before she could share Starr's news with Sean, she spotted a white tornado coming toward them. "I think our time here has ended, Dear," she predicted as they were scooped away.

Deposited at the Crystal Castle's boat dock, they moved to sit in the very comfortable chairs there. "I was just thinking about our dock, Sean," she commented, "and here we are."

"Just before the tornado grabbed us," Sean remarked, "I thought you were about to tell me something."

"I was," she affirmed, "and it's going to be a shocker. Starr had just finished letting me know that, in addition to Candace, I am also hosting a set of fraternal twins!"

"BOTH of you!" exclaimed Sean. "How grand!"…the number FOUR flashing through his mind. "The other twins in our family were all identical, but this time both sets will be fraternal. I wonder why?"

"I have no idea," Tamara replied, "I guess we'll just have to wait and see."

Looking up, Sean noticed Rogere and Elsa walking toward them. "Would you like to take a ride?" asked Rogere…"to celebrate the good news?"

"You know?" Sean was surprised.

"You will find that we know everything concerning the two of you," assured Elsa. "It's part of our responsibilities."

"Then can you share any intel about why both sets of twins to enter our family will be fraternal, rather than identical like all the rest?" Sean asked.

"It's an unusual situation," responded Elsa, "But the Creator Being has not told us anything about that."

Terra suddenly appeared and sat next to Tamara. "One thing I've learned about the Creator Being is that everything has a reason. We'll just have to be patient."

"Actually, it's one more change to deal with," Rogere pointed out, "in addition to wondering about possible accelerated growth and Generational status!"

"Since we have more questions than answers," commented Rogere, taking the wheel, "I'm going to get this boat moving!"

Elsa suddenly had an armful of sweaters and passed them out. "It can get chilly on the water, even when the weather is ideal," she explained.

Accepting the sweaters gratefully, Tamara and Sean snuggled together as their two chairs became a couch. They prepared to enjoy their first boat ride since relocating to the Castle. Terra decided to remain aboard and enjoy the experience. It had been a long time since she had been on a boat.

Elsa stood at Rogere's side as he steered the boat down the river. The blue sky morphed into a canopy of stars and soft music emerged to accompany their journey. It seemed that a lovely evening was ahead for everyone.

Chapter 6
From Palace to Castle

Queen Candace and Cecil said farewell to the rest of the family, deciding to also stroll through the Garden. They were hoping to catch up with her parents, who had appeared to be heading toward the boat dock. But when they arrived at the dock, it was empty.

Disappointed, Candace suggested that they sit and rest a bit. Taking seats, they didn't look up to see the white tornado approaching. Then it was too late and they were scooped up and deposited at another, unfamiliar dock.

"What happened?" she cried, "and where are we?"

"I don't know," admitted Cecil. "Nothing looks familiar to me. What brought us here?"

"It felt like a strong wind," Candace guessed. "Wait…I know what it was. In the past, a white tornado transported my parents to the Crystal Castle. Perhaps that's where we are."

"But why?" asked Cecil. "I don't understand."

Suddenly, Terra was at their side. She looked puzzled. "I was just enjoying a lovely boat ride…and now I'm back at the dock! I admit to being confused."

"You're confused?" Candace exclaimed. "We were trying to find my parents and were unsuccessful. Now we're here—presumably at the Crystal Castle, if I'm correct. Do you know what's going on?"

"I was relaxing on a boat with your parents when I was transported here," explained Terra. "Look, I see the boat approaching now—but it had just left this dock...and now it's back!"

"Mother, you disappeared," cried Tamara. "Why are we back at the dock?"

"Candace and Cecil were brought here by a white tornado," answered Terra. "None of us know what is happening."

"But Mother," complained Tamara, "You always know everything!"

"Not this time," informed Terra. "I detect the Creator Being's hand in this."

"That's a good observation, Terra," said a strange voice.

As the boat docked, there was a shimmer in the air on the dock and a mysterious figure appeared. "My name is Bugle. I am a messenger from the Creator Being and a temporary replacement for you as Head Watcher."

"What!" cried Terra. "Why? What have I done?"

"Nothing," Bugle assured her. "You have been an excellent Head Watcher. But the Creator Being needs you here at the Crystal Castle until both your daughter and granddaughter have delivered their twin babes. These babes are very unique and special…and are essential to our plans for the changing universe.

"I will be in constant communication with you during your stay here. Your responsibility will be to transmit the intel I share with you to the present Guardians of the Castle and the parents of these special babes. Because Time is different here, no one back in Marinea will miss you."

Candace looked distraught. "Even with the difference in Time, my kingdom will have no Ruler. My daughter Joy needs to be notified that she has been activated as Queen-Designate!" she insisted.

Bugle stood silently, as if listening. "Very well," he stated. "Terra, you are authorized to make it so and then return here immediately."

As everyone watched, Terra vanished.

*   *   *   *   *

When the three couples regained their composure, they were back inside the Crystal Castle and about to have another dinner. Rogere and Elsa tried to cast calming spells, but were largely unsuccessful. The tension at their table was huge.

When Terra had vanished, Bugle had also disappeared. The two Queens, past and present, and their Consorts were visibly upset. A flash of light, and Terra had returned.

"I was able to pass the intel to Joy," she related. "She doesn't understand what is happening either, but was willing to accept her duty. She's quite a young lady; you should all be proud."

"But what about her Ship?" asked Candace. "She was about to take it on a training mission."

"The mission has been temporarily delayed," answered Terra. "We have to trust that the Time difference between here and there will smooth things out. Now, let's try and relax and enjoy dinner."

It was amazing. Even though they had just finished dinner in Marinea, the Time difference allowed their appetites to reset. Also, food prepared in the Castle seemed to stimulate other appetites, such as happiness and the desire to rest. It wasn't long before they crawled into bed, snuggled, and were soon fast asleep. When they awoke the next morning, they felt relaxed and alert— but not anxious or fearful. The Castle had worked its magic overnight.

Chapter 7
Back at the Palace

Joy had gone through most of the paperwork in the Royal Office. It wasn't the most interesting project, she decided. She had a new respect for what a Queen must do as part of her duties…and hoped that she would never be responsible on a full-time basis.

In the few weeks that she had served as Queen, she had learned several things: Royal paperwork was BORING…and she hoped her mother would live a long time because becoming Queen was definitely NOT a desire of hers personally. Joy loved being the Captain of a Spaceship. That was where her future lay.

At least, one positive outcome had made this chore more palatable: Nolan was helping her since he was also grounded by these recent circumstances. It was rare that they could spend quality time together…and it felt nice.

As she continued to chip away at the pile of paperwork before her, a bright light announced the arrival of a Super Child. Looking up, Joy noticed that there were several Super Children standing before her: her parents and her grandparents…holding babes! And Terra was there, too!

Was she dreaming? It had only been a couple of weeks since they left. Then she remembered the Time difference between the Crystal Castle and the planet Akura.

Both Joy and Nolan stood and moved quickly to welcome and hug their family members—and fuss over the babes!

"I know there are Time differences at work, but seeing all of you is beyond amazing!" Joy cried. Nolan nodded his agreement. Terra was smiling broadly while she conjured up some chairs so everyone could sit.

"Probably more amazing than you can imagine," added Tamara. "These four—and remember what I've said about FOUR—were not only born early, but VERY early. Joy, you and your children all accelerated your growth. But these little ones outdid all of you."

"Once we arrived at the Crystal Castle," continued Sean, "it was only a couple of weeks before they demanded to be born!"

Candace added more details. "When they slipped out of our bodies, they were the size of a small mouse. Within minutes, they reached the size you see here and Terra teleported us to the Royal Office."

"We're not sure if they're still growing or at what pace," Cecil commented. "We still watch them closely."

Joy chanted softly and touched the babes' foreheads. "The number 12 appeared!" she exclaimed. "Their powers will be extraordinary."

Another flash of light and Starr joined them. Looking closely at the babes, he observed, "They are still growing and may be adults before the rise of the next moon. Shamous is upstairs in the Classroom, preparing some temporary beds for them. Shall we relocate there?"

Terra nodded and teleported the group to the Classroom. Not knowing what size he was dealing with, Shamous had created four oversized cribs with sides. But the beds could accommodate even fully-grown adults.

Once the babes were placed in the beds, they all began to cry. Starr turned to the new parents and advised, "They wish to be put to bed together, two by two." Shamous waved his hands and the four beds merged into two. The crying stopped.

Shamous waved his hand once again and a security bubble surrounded each bed. "Just in case they figure out how to leave the beds," he explained.

"One more thing," he added as he clothed the babes in different colors and styles. The girls wore solid colors; the boys wore stripes. Tamara's babes' clothes were red; the clothes of

Candace's babes were green. As a final touch, two wardrobes appeared against the wall, filled with additional clothes and diapers for the babes, in the appropriate colors.

"The clothes are spelled to automatically increase in size as the babes progress," Shamous commented. Addressing Tamara, he asked whether she and Sean would be returning immediately to the Crystal Castle with their babes. Everyone looked at Terra for an answer to that question. She answered that in one moon's time, she would return to move them to the Castle. Until then, they were being allowed to remain in the Palace.

Smiles all around, a family reunion began to take place…until Starr called out, "Look, the babes are standing!"

*   *   *   *   *

When the next moon rose, the family members gathered in the Classroom and revisited the events that had occurred since the two sets of parents and babes had arrived at the Palace.

There had been many changes surrounding the family. Tamara and Sean had named their twins Scarlett and Pepper, reflecting the color of their clothes. Also thinking about the color of the clothing, Candace and Cecil called their twins Fernne and Forrest. Each twin's name contained a double letter, emphasizing their status as twins.

Both sets of twins had managed to grow at a disturbing rate. As the new moon approached, each twin was almost halfway to adult size.

It was clear that the 'babes' did not want to be separated from each other. What would they do to keep it from happening?

Chapter 8
"Twin Power"

When it was time to return to the Crystal Castle, Tamara and Sean couldn't find their babes. They asked Starr to use his Generation 10 abilities, but he was not successful.

"We can't return to the Castle without them," stated Tamara firmly.

"Of course not," agreed Sean. Then one of his birds landed on his shoulder with a message in it's beak. "This is a proposal for negotiation!" he exclaimed.

"What are the opening conditions?" asked Tamara.

"They are willing to accompany us until full-growth is attained," read Sean. "As soon as it is, they want assurances that they will be allowed to rejoin the other twins at the Palace."

Tamara sighed, "I have to admit that the proposal is reasonable. How do you feel, Sean?"

"I reluctantly agree," he said. He wrote a response on the proposal and released the bird. Within minutes, Scarlett and Pepper were standing in front of their parents.

"You do realize, Mama," began Scarlett, "that achieving full-growth may not be a long time away?"

Tamara thought privately, "*You may be underestimating the power of the Castle, my Dear.*"

She didn't realize that one of Scarlett's powers was accessing private thought. But she would soon find out.

Parents and children held hands as they watched the white tornado approach. The other set of twins observed from behind a tree. "They'll be back soon," whispered Fernne.

"I know," responded Forestt.

*   *   *   *   *

The white tornado deposited Tamara, Sean and their twins on the Crystal Castle dock. As they were walking back to the Castle, Tamara stopped and grabbed Sean's arm. "Look at the twins," she whispered.

Sean shifted his glance from Tamara to the twins and whispered back, "They're growing again! It won't be long before they are adult size and we have promised to send them back to the Palace!"

"Why is it that we have never been able to enjoy our children as babes?" Tamara began to complain.

"Perhaps you should ask your mother that question," recommended Sean. "She seems to know the mind of the Creator Being."

"I had hoped that the Castle would slow down their growth," continued Tamara, "but it seems to be helping them grow."

Terra joined them on the walk. "No one can predict what the Castle will do," she said. "But I have a feeling that these twins have a special relationship with the Castle…and the Castle obeys the Creator Being."

Tamara decided to take Sean's advice, "Mother, do you know why we haven't been able to enjoy our children as babes?"

"I do not," admitted Terra, "but I have wondered that myself. I'll be right back." and she disappeared.

As Tamara and Sean neared the Castle, Terra returned. "The Creator Being told me that your life path does not include parenting. You are destined for greater things, which is why you are now here."

"So, procreating but not parenting," Sean murmured. "That's quite a mouthful. We have done a lot of parenting through advice, however."

"Yes," admitted Terra, "Your advice has been important, but it hasn't taken much actual time to do that. Your mission is quite different than that of other parents."

"Looking back," commented Tamara, "I can see the truth in what you're saying—even though I don't have to like it! So, how would you describe our mission?"

Looking deeply into her daughter's eyes, Terra replied, "To save the universe, my Dear. And the two sets of twins that are just now reaching adulthood, will be instrumental in helping you do that." Then Terra vanished.

Concern on her face, Tamara squeezed Sean's hand and hurried her pace. "I want to talk to our Guardians," she stressed.

Reaching the Castle, they found the Guardians waiting for them. "We need to talk," insisted Tamara, picturing in her mind the table in the Garden where they had many of their meals.

That thought deposited them in chairs by the table. "You have learned well how to move in the Castle," praised Elsa.

"Please tell us what you know of our mission," ordered Tamara.

"I see that Terra has been consulting with the Creator Being," commented Rogere. "Very well. Let me begin."

*   *   *   *   *

When Rogere had finished explaining, Tamara sank back in her chair and clasped Sean's hand. "What you have described is a frightening scenario, Rogere," she sighed. "How are we to deal with it?"

Rogere replied, "You will know when the time comes." Then he and Elsa disappeared.

Chapter 9
The Mission

At dinner that evening, Tamara and Sean spoke to the twins about their growth pattern.

"How close to full adult size do you think you are now?" asked Tamara.

Scarlett blushed and answered, "Really close, Mama."

"And you promised to let us return to the Palace once we achieve it," reminded Pepper.

"Why are you so eager to return?" inquired Sean.

"We miss Fernne and Forrest," replied Pepper. "All through our childhood, they were with us."

Tamara commented, "That childhood you speak of was quite short. The four of you grew as quickly as you could manage it. What was the hurry?"

Scarlet's cheeks turned red, "I don't know. But we felt that it was important to become adult as soon as possible."

"Were you getting instructions from someone or somewhere?" Sean pressed.

"Da, it was a bit strange," admitted Pepper. "When we would fall asleep at night, I heard music that had funny lyrics chanting 'grow, grow'. Then, when we awoke in the morning, we were bigger."

"So you weren't doing it purposefully?" asked Tamara.

"Not really, Mama," Scarlett claimed. "We loved being with you and Da."

"Did Fernne and Forrest have the same experience?" asked Sean.

"Yes," admitted Pepper. "We talked about it a lot. None of us understood what was happening."

"Why didn't you tell us?" demanded Sean. "Didn't you trust us?"

"Some of the lyrics included the word 'secret'," shared Scarlet. "We were afraid to tell you."

Tamara called for the Guardians, who appeared promptly. "Did you overhear our conversation?" she demanded.

"Yes, we did," said Rogere. "We knew something was disturbing them, but not what."

"Am I correct that all of this took place during the one moon's time that we were all together in the Palace?" pressed Tamara.

"You are correct," admitted Rogere. "We had no control over you while you were away from the Castle."

Tamara sent an urgent summons to her mother, who appeared immediately. Terra looked worried. She glanced at the two Guardians, who also seemed distressed.

"It seems that the mission I described to you has already begun," confessed Rogere. "It is important that you return to Akura, with your twins. That is where the confrontation will occur."

"What confrontation?" asked Terra. "What have I not been told?" She faded from sight as the white tornado scooped up Tamara, Sean and the twins.

*   *   *   *   *

Landing on the Palace boat dock, rather unceremoniously, they found Candace and Cecil waiting for them, with their twins. "What is happening?" asked a frightened Candace. "Our twins just demanded to come to the dock. Is something amiss?"

Now that the two families were together, Terra rejoined them. "Yes, I'm afraid so. Please sit down and we will try to chart a path forward."

Once they were all seated comfortably, Terra continued, "Candace, you just received a mysterious document. Do you have it with you?"

"I do," Candace said, "I was just about to open it. Shall I do so?"

"Yes, please," responded Terra. "I have just spoken to the Creator Being. The contents of that document are a challenge to our planet."

Candace carefully opened the sealed document, handling it as if it would explode! She silently read it, then began to read it aloud. After doing so, Candace concluded, "It would seem that the document has been somehow sent from another galaxy, not ours. The authors have ambitions to control not only their own galaxy, but the universe itself. They claim to have been watching our development on Akura and now view us as a threat to those ambitions.

"Therefore," she summarized, "they challenge us to a series of games—winner take all! Apparently, they view war as a useless destroyer of resources and prefer to compete in a more 'civilized' manner.

"However, if we don't agree to their terms, they profess to have superior weaponry and will destroy our planet."

When she had finished, there was shock on everyone's face.

*   *   *   *   *

Sean frowned, "We definitely need more intel before we can decide our path forward." A flash of light and Starr had joined them.

46

"Savvy and I will do some future journeys to see what options are out there. Please don't do anything rash until we return," he advised. "If you are contacted again, try to delay any commitments." And Starr vanished.

Chapter 10

Savvy and Starr

Standing together at the arc of Time, Savvy and Starr prepared to move into it. They would travel a short distance, step off, and assess their surroundings. Unsure of what they would discover, they held hands so that they would stay connected.

At the first stop, they looked around and noticed little change. Teleporting to the Palace, they watched Candace and Cyril appearing worried as they read some documents.

Teleporting to Security Force Headquarters, they observed Sean rallying the troops in anticipation of an imminent attack. Suddenly the sky was filled with Space vehicles that were primed to discharge weapons.

Back at the arc of Time, they moved forward again, getting off at a second stop. The view was terrifying...it was total devastation. There was no sign of life.

Savvy gestured to the side, pointing to a different stream of Time. They hopped aboard and exited almost immediately. At this location, everything looked serene. There was no sign of attack.

Sean and Jon were passing out some strange weapons that were not familiar. When they moved on to a second stop, those same weapons were being used in a fire fight…and the Security Force was losing.

Starr pointed to a third stream of Time and they hopped over to it. They landed in the Control Room of Explorer 3—Joy's Ship. The two sets of twins born most recently were there, studying some papers. Peering over the twins' shoulders, they saw instructions for some games. Could those be the rules for the competition proposed by the challengers?

Deciding to stay in this stream of Time, they jumped forward to the next stop. They were in the middle of a huge arena that was not familiar to either of them. Listening to some spectators, they were unable to understand the language.

Looking down at the playing field, they recognized the two sets of twins, who were facing some opponents. Those opponents were clearly from an alien race and were armed with strange weapons. However, the twins were able to adequately defend themselves.

"*Clearly,*" commented Starr, "*this is the best stream to take. The twins absolutely need to be involved.*"

"*Agreed,*" stressed Savvy. "*But we don't know how they are managing to overcome those aliens.*"

"*True,*" said Starr, "*but this is the only positive stream that we have seen. We need to report it.*"

Stepping away from the arc of Time, they teleported back to the Palace and the Royal Office. Sean, Jon, Tamara, Candace and Cyril were waiting there, eager to learn what the siblings had found out.

"We checked out three different streams of Time," began Savvy, "and only one displayed any hope. That stream involved both sets of recent twins, who were actively participating in the challenge presented by the aliens."

"We didn't see the results of that stream," added Starr. "but we did find out that the other two streams ended in disaster."

"So your recommendation is that we accept the challenge in the document we received?" asked Candace.

"It was the best option we encountered," admitted Savvy. "And the two sets of twins seem to be central to any possibility of a good outcome."

"Very well," said Candace. "I will respond to the document immediately. Hopefully, more details will be forthcoming." She turned and went to her desk. As she finished her reply and signed it, the paper shimmered and disappeared.

"That's unnerving," mentioned Tamara. "Their technology is certainly impressive."

"From this point on," added Sean, "I advise including both sets of twins in all our discussions. If Savvy and Starr are correct, they are key to our future."

Tamara nodded and sent a mental summons to the twins, who arrived in a flash of light. She opened her mind to them in an effort to bring them up-to-date. Expecting them to react with worry, fear, or at least concern, she was surprised that the four twins smiled broadly and looked eager to meet the challenge.

"Am I misinterpreting how you feel about this challenge?" she asked.

Scarlett giggled and replied, "Not at all, Mama. We have been sharing intel about our abilities with each other…and we aren't at all intimidated."

Fernne added another perspective, "These aliens may have been spying on us for some time, but we are too new. They won't have any intel about us. That's our advantage."

"Are you willing to share intel about your abilities with us?" asked Sean.

"Sorry, Da," replied Pepper. "It wouldn't be wise to do so at this time. We can't risk any intel being picked up by them. Also, we respectively decline meeting with you for the same reason. But don't worry…we'll know what you decide or plan to do." And the four twins disappeared.

"Well!" Sean almost laughed. "I guess we've been told. But I have to agree with their logic. I think we should be as careful, so I recommend that our meetings be held only in a secure facility. The Force has just developed a state-of-the-art location, which is not known to anyone. I will mentally send directions to all of you and advise complete silence regarding this challenge outside that facility and the use of mental communication only within it."

Nodding soberly, the group dispersed and headed to the Private Dining Room for dinner.

Chapter 11
The Aliens' Response

The next day, when Candace and Cyril entered the Royal Office, they saw a response from the aliens on the Queen's desk.

Details regarding the challenge were clearly articulated. No more than four players from each side would be allowed. Identical weapons would be provided at the site of the games. There would be no time allocated for planning or strategizing. The games would be conducted in silence and all actions would be impromptu—and could be offense or defense, or both. Each team would have fireballs to move from one end of the field to the goal at the other end, where there were buckets of water. The first team to deposit a fireball in a bucket of water would be victorious. No injuries would be treated.

The game would be winner-take-all.

Candace was horrified. This 'game' was brutal. Presumably, the alien team would have experience playing such a 'game'. That was inherently unfair—and there was no way to protest.

She was beginning to tremble and Cyril moved to comfort her. As he did so, they were teleported to the Force's mysterious secure facility. Fortunately, Cyril had grabbed the alien document so it was transported with them.

When they arrived, they saw that the entire planning group was present—but not the twins.

"Where are the twins?" Candace cried silently. *"They have to know what they will be up against!"*

"We have to believe that they know what they are doing," soothed Sean. *"Let's mentally discuss this new document."*

The morning was spent in exchanging mental thoughts that ranged from logic to panic. At lunchtime, food appeared on the table…closely followed by a new message from the aliens.

This new message gave details for arrival at the site of the competition. They were told to gather at a specific point on Marinea, where the aliens would transport them to the 'game' site. The place was listed; the time was next day at the same time as right now.

The team members looked at each other around the table. There was an atmosphere of fear and panic in the room. Tamara and Sean studied Terra's expression, which was mixed. She held up one finger, as if to say 'wait' and then vanished.

When she returned in a few moments, she chanted a powerful privacy spell that created a silver haze—which turned into a translucent bubble. *"I consulted the Creator Being, who allowed me to produce this additional layer of privacy,"* she explained mentally. *"I'm hopeful that it works as expected. I was disturbed that the alien message could breach this secure facility."*

She looked directly at Tamara and Sean, commenting, *"This is why the Creator Being promoted you to Super Being status. You are needed to save our planet from these alien insurgents. A response has already been sent to the aliens that insists on two coaches being approved to accompany the four players to the 'game' site."*

Another message from the aliens appeared on the table, agreeing to that modification of the instructions.

Terra handed whistles on cords to Tamara and Sean. *"Wear these whistles around your necks. When you need a truly private conversation with the twins, blow the whistle and a privacy bubble will deploy."*

"Are you certain that the whistles will work effectively in an alien environment?" asked Sean.

"*I am hopeful,*" admitted Terra.

A sudden flash of light and the four twins appeared in the room. "*They will work,*" promised Forrest. "*We have seen it. Thank you for insisting on our having two coaches. Their advice will be very important.*" And the twins vanished.

"*As I said,*" Sean laughed, "*We need to trust that the twins are aware of what we discuss in this room.*"

Tamara was rubbing her temples. Her family realized that she was having another one of her famous headaches. Candace was doing the same. Terra put her hands on their heads and a feeling of peace and calm flowed through their bodies. They thanked Terra and reached for some of the provided lunch.

Tension in the room was high and not likely to dissipate until the alien threat had been defeated. Gazing at each other, Tamara and Sean were wondering what advice they could possibly provide to the twins that would be meaningful in this dangerous situation.

Then they heard Terra's voice in their minds, reminding them of the many challenges they had faced during Tamara's reign—and repelled successfully. Sean squeezed Tamara's hand and smiled. She returned the smile and put her head on his shoulder. Terra was right; they were a formidable team—exactly what was needed!

Chapter 12
The Game

The next day, at the appointed place and time, the four twins were joined by their two coaches. A flash of light and they vanished.

*　　*　　*　　*　　*

At an unknown part of the universe, they reappeared in what looked like a sports stadium. The stands were full of screaming 'fans', some of whom looked human. Others did resemble the opposing 'team' of four multi-legged beings on the other side of the field. But there were clusters of fans with still different appearances.

Sean blew his whistle and the twins huddled with him in the privacy bubble. *"Don't worry, Papa,"* soothed Pepper, *"We have seen them before. We know their strategy and have observed their game plan. Hopefully, they still know nothing about us."*

"Don't panic if you see us play like underdogs," added Scarlet. *"Disinformation is an offensive skill."*

Sean nodded and released the bubble.

They were greeted by a humanoid-appearing being who seemed to be a referee and directed them to benches in the end zone that was across from that of the 'home team'. Fireballs were piled up next to the benches in both end zones. Looking down to the other end zone, they spied buckets of water. But to get to that location, the twins would have to traverse what looked like an obstacle course, complete with water hazards.

Tamara and Sean asked the twins to be seated on the benches. After Sean blew his whistle, creating the privacy bubble, they began to transmit positive mental messages. The messages basically told the twins to trust themselves. *"You know what you're capable of,"* emphasized Tamara. *"Rely on those skills and the skills of your teammates. Don't let your opponents drain your confidence. YOU CAN DO THIS!"*

Sean applauded when Tamara was finished, but he had noticed that, during her speech, the four twins were smiling and interacting with each other. He wondered why.

A rocket in the middle of the field ignited and roared into the sky. The twins rose and stood on the line in their end zone. They seemed to know that the game was beginning.

At the other end of the field, the opposing team was also at the ready. Each team member held a fireball—without being burned! Now they began to scamper toward the twins' end zone— very quickly, since they had all those legs.

While all this was going on, the twins breathed on their hands, coating them with ice, and picked up their fireballs. They began to run toward their opponents…and leaped over them! One more leap and the twins were at the far end zone. Depositing the fireballs in the buckets, they raised their hands in victory!

But as they turned around, the twins saw that their opponents had also been successful. It was a draw!

A piece of paper fluttered down in front of Tamara. It contained instructions for Round Two. *"Round Two?"* she asked. *"I thought there was just one game. What happened?"*

"No, Mama," explained Scarlett. *"There are several Rounds, each one with different rules. When we were on the arc of Time, there were several iterations of the Game, each one with different numbers of Games. The competition didn't end until our opponents won a Game."*

"Then what happened?" asked Sean. *"If our side won six Games and the opponents won one, was the competition ended in our favor?"*

"No, Papa," answered Pepper. *"Then it was declared that the opponents were victorious."*

"So our side lost?" Tamara exclaimed.

"According to their interpretation of the rules," admitted Fernne. *"That's why we kept rewinding the competition on the arc of Time."*

"*Eventually they caught on,*" laughed Forest. "*And they officially called the Games over…in a draw. It will take a while to play out in real Time, but we are confident of the outcome.*"

"*How confident?*" pressed Sean. "*Will they still be a threat to our planet?*"

"*We don't know,*" admitted Scarlet. "*We stopped watching when the game was declared a draw.*"

"*But we did find out one thing,*" Pepper boasted. "*This is the planet that Nolan escaped from. The multi-legged creatures may not be residents; they might be like pets on Akura—but much more intelligent.*"

"*Since there are a lot of them in the stands, they must be more important—somewhat like a second species of resident,*" Tamara suggested. "*We need much more intel. I'm assuming that you need to engage the arc of Time fully before we will be released from this planet. Do you agree?*"

The four twins nodded vigorously and prepared to do just that. Tamara and Sean continued to watch the game unfold—but were very relieved when the draw was announced by the referee, who then walked over to speak with them.

"Do not be misled by the calling of a draw," the referee

said. "We are releasing you for the moment while we study the results of the competition. You may be required to return for further games in the future." Turning around, the referee returned to confer with the home team.

The four twins clasped hands, including those of Tamara and Sean, and chanted an unfamiliar spell. They were suddenly airborne overlooking the arc of Time, which was visible beneath them. Another spell facilitated the ability to teleport and, suddenly, they were back in Marinea, in the Palace.

Chapter 13
Post-Game Analysis

The next day, Tamara convened the Defense Team, the Kingdom Delegates and the SC/United members in the Private Dining Room for a debriefing. Sunan had also been invited.

The two sets of twins were present, since they were personally involved with the 'game.' Prior to the meeting, they had deliberately journeyed to the arc of Time to gain more intel. Questions began to flow and Tamara turned the meeting over to the twins.

When the debriefing had ended, there was a period of complete silence while everyone attempted to absorb what they had heard.

The first startling piece of new intel that the twins added to Tamara's presentation concerned the residents of the alien planet. Scarlett spoke first, "We noticed that the stands of the stadium were filled with many different types of beings. There was no dominant species, such as we are used to here on Akura. We were puzzled about that, which is why we returned to the arc of Time when we returned home."

Pepper added, "We traveled a good distance into both the past and the future, trying to figure out why that was so."

Forrest chimed in, "And then we closely watched a small group change right in front of us. Those aliens are shape-shifters! They can alter their appearance at will."

"Which is pretty handy when you're trying to win a competition!" commented Fernne. "You can pick a body type that would be best suited to the conditions."

"And that's why we were pitted against an opposing team with many legs enabling speed," added Forrest.

"Since we were released conditionally, with the caveat that we could be recalled," Scarlett suggested, "we are assuming that they are deciding how best to face us next time."

"What we don't know, no matter how far into the future we looked," complained Pepper, "is how—or if—we can win this stupid game."

A sigh of frustration echoed around the room. A related question came from the back of the group, "Do you know what the penalty is if you lose the game?"

"Yes," admitted Scarlet. "Our planet is forfeit, so that is not an option."

A universal gasp could be heard, followed by another question: "And if you win?"

"Apparently," said Pepper, "that has never happened to them before. They pretend that it can't possibly be a result. I think the game is their way of expanding territory."

"Yet you were able to extricate yourselves this time by rewinding Time," asked a Super Child. "Is that not correct?"

"Yes, that's true," Scarlett nodded.

"So why can't you just keep doing that until they tire of the effort?" another Super Child questioned.

More questions followed, but no concrete solutions appeared. A soft voice asked, "On your Time travels, did you come across anything that might be a threat to their planet's existence?"

"No," admitted Forrest, "but we weren't really looking for it either. I think another Time journey might be indicated." The twins nodded at each other and vanished.

Tamara and Sean looked at each other and laughed. "If enthusiasm and persistence are factors, I think we have nothing to worry about!" Tamara smiled.

Suddenly the twins were back. At first, Tamara was puzzled, but then she remembered that they could use the arc of Time to return to the exact moment they left. The four twins were smiling and looked pleased with themselves.

"Pepper was right," exclaimed Scarlett. "The governing

authority IS using the game as a way of seizing territory. Everyone we talked with was very negative about their practices."

"And they have pretty much run out of new land to seize," reported Forrest. "That is why they are looking around other galaxies for possible victims."

"One more thing," added Fernne. "There's a rumor that their planet is running out of water and they are seeking a whole new planet to occupy. We think that's where we come in."

Sean saw Tamara's face light up. "That could be our way in," she cried. "We've done this before—finding a new virgin planet for a predatory and needy planet. It worked well for Planet X. Let's see if we can initiate some diplomatic contact here—shall we call it Planet G for Game?. Sean, do you have any available birds?"

*   *   *   *   *

The next day, Joy returned to the arc of Time. She had decided to take control of this part of the mission and not risk the four twins. She had a few days until Explorer 3 would need its Captain and she had a lot of experience with traveling the arc.

Finding a promising exit ramp leading toward Planet G, she aimed the birds from Sean directly at the planet. Hopefully, they would reach the planet safely and be taken to whoever ruled the planet. Chuckling, she thought, "There was no Time to waste.

About the Author

After doing academic writing during my 20 years as Professor at the University of Wisconsin-Madison, I retired to Hawai'i in 1999. A decade later, I began being aware of an interesting fantasy story line in my mind and began writing it soon after. It was an occasional hobby for another decade and then the book became impatient with me and began to seriously nudge me. Since I began "listening" to the book, the writing has been a fun and all-encompassing part of my life.

I have completed 12 books in my Crystal Saga Series 1 and 12 books in Crystal Saga Series 2. I have completed books 1 through 12 in my Crystal Saga Series 3 and I have now completed Books 1 and 2, 3 and 4 in Series 4 with more to come. Expect more adventures soon.

Crystal Saga Series 1 by
D. E. Weingand

Scan the QR Code with Your Cell Phone to Order Books. Or go to LuLu.com, Amazon.com, Barnsandnoble.com and many other outlets.

Crystal Saga Series 2 by
D. E. Weingand

Crystal Saga Series 3 by
D. E. Weingand

Crystal Saga Series 4 by
D. E. Weingand

Book 1 — Defense = Offense

Book 2 — Interplanetary Conflict

Book 3 — The New Order

Book 4 — Adapting to Change

Coming Soon

Book 5 — The Game. . .Round 2

Book 6 — TBA

www.ingramcontent.com/pod-product-compliance
Lightning Source LLC
Chambersburg PA
CBHW071216260626
47162CB00004B/1310